Ma Waho Aku I Ke Kohola
Nā Moʻolelo o Maui I Ka Honua

Beyond the Reef
Stories of Maui in the World

Ma Waho Aku I Ke Kohola
Nā Moʻolelo o Maui I Ka Honua

Beyond the Reef
Stories of Maui in the World

Wayne Moniz

Pūnāwai Press
1812 Nani Street
Wailuku, Maui
Hawai`i 96793

Copyright © 2011 by Wayne Moniz
Cover Art copyright © 2011 by Joseph Aspell
Author photo by Nagamine Photo Studio Inc.
Printed in the United States of America

Distributed in America and Worldwide by Pūnāwai Press and Amazon Books
For more about the book and author, Google: *Beyond the Reef: Stories of Maui in the World/Wayne Moniz*

Beyond the Reef : Stories of Maui in the World = Ma Waho Aku I Ke Kohola: Nā Mo`olelo o Maui I Ka Honua/ Wayne Moniz. –Wailuku, Hawai`i: Pūnāwai Press, c2011

ISBN: 978-0-9791507-3-9

Includes glossary of Hawaiian, pidgin, and ethnic words, and locations

1. Hawaiian—Fiction. 2. Maui (Hawai`i)—Fiction. 3. Hawaiians—Fiction 4. Hawai`i—Poetry. 5. Short Stories I. Title. II. Title: Ma Waho Aku I Ke Kohola: Nā Mo`olelo o Maui I Ka Honua.

~ CONTENTS ~

MAHALO xii

PRONOUNCING HAWAIIAN WORDS xiv

PREFACE xv

I WALKED WITH THE NIGHT MARCHERS 1
Ua Hele Au Me Nā Huaka`i Pō
GHOST STORY WAIKAPŪ THE PRESENT
A curious student is caught up in the world of spirit warriors.
Dedicated to Boy Kana`e and `Ohana and
Chuck and Marlene Powell and `Ohana

A DAY AT THE PALACE /
A NIGHT AT THE OPERA 15
He Lā I Ka Hale Ali`i / He Pō i Ke Keaka Mele
COMEDY HONOLULU 1881
Liliu`okalani is trying to write an opera, and a mongoose is on the loose.
Dedicated to Rodger and Georgia Bridgen and `Ohana
and Deb Peyton and `Ohana

THE FIRES OF PU`UO`UMI 29
Nā Ahi o Pu`uo`umi
INSPIRATIONAL WAIĀPUKA, BIG ISLAND 1865
WAILUKU, MAUI 1873
*An assumption that Damien encountered a leper
on the Big Island.*
Dedicated to Miriam and Robert Chipp and `Ohana
and Joseph Aspell and `Ohana

v

THE BIG L 45
Ka Lā Nui
CRIME LAHAINA and PĀ`IA 1938
Two inept thieves become Maui's first bank robbers.
Dedicated to Dave Peyton and `Ohana
and Joe, Julie and Helen Cecchi and `Ohana

THE TRAIL TO MĀNĀ 67
Ke Ala i Mānā
WESTERN
`ULUPALAKUA, MAUI/ PU`UWA`AWA`A, BIG ISLAND/
PU`UHUE, BIG ISLAND
SAN FRANCISCO, CALIFORNIA/ CHEYENNE, WYOMING
1843 – THE PRESENT
The severed limb of a hard working cowboy, Eben Low, eventually leads to accolades for Ikua Purdy, Hawaii's champion paniolo.
Dedicated to Tom and Michele Allen and `Ohana,
the Low and Purdy `Ohana,
and all cowboys past and present

THE TEENAGE CREATURE FROM THE BLACK LAGOON 85
Ka Mea Ola `Ōpio no Ka Kaikohola `Ele`ele
COMING OF AGE WAILUKU/KAHULUI/KĪHEI 1963
A prankish plot and a love affair are hatched by teens in 1960s Maui.
Dedicated to Julia Kaeha Hall, Jimmy Souza, Karen Andrade Stovall,
Paulette Souza Davis and `Ohana

FOR THE ROSE OF THE CHIEFS 101
Ha`alilio's Quest For Sovereignty
No Ka Loke O Nā Ali`i
Ka `Imi O Ha`alilio No Ka Ea
TRAGEDY
HONOLULU, O`AHU/LAHAINA, MAUI/WASHINGTON, D.C./
NEW HAVEN, CONNECTICUT/PARIS, FRANCE/
BOSTON, MASSACHUSETTS/THE ATLANTIC OCEAN
1823 - 1845
Kamehameha III sends his closest friend on a journey to attain sovereignty.
Dedicated to Laurel Douglass and Guy Gaumont and `Ohana
and Val and Oliver Dukelow and `Ohana

ON THE WINGS OF BLUEBIRDS 121
In Nā Hulu `Ekekeu O Nā Manu Uli
SPORTS
WAILUKU, MAUI/CORONA DEL MAR, CALIFORNIA/
WAIKĪKĪ, O`AHU
1936 - 1920 - 1917
Duke Kahanamoku visits Wailuku and tells his life saving story.
Dedicated to Val and Dan Bridges and `Ohana
and Tom and Laurie Dankwardt and `Ohana

NOTES ON THE SHORT STORIES 131

KAONA AND OTHER MELE 141

THE WHALE 143
Ke Koholā
Dedicated to Clarence Butch Moniz

THE ULUA 144
Ka Ulua
Dedicated to Stan Moniz

THE `ULA `ULA 145
Ka `Ula `Ula
Dedicated to Steve Moniz

THE MOI 146
Ka Moi
Dedicated to Eddie Moniz

THE KŌLEA 147
Ke Kōlea
Dedicated to John Moniz

THE KALO 148
Ke Kalo
Dedicated to Johnny Texeira

THE KOA 149
Ke Koa
Dedicated to Jerome Keli`iho`omalu

THE WHITE RAIN OF HĀNA 150
Ka Ua Kea O Hāna
Dedicated to Pekelo Cosma

GLOSSARY: Hawaiian/English 151

GLOSSARY: Pidgin/English 156

GLOSSARY: Ethnic/English 158

GLOSSARY: Sites and Locations 160

MAPS 166
Hawaiian Islands/Maui/Big Island

BY THE SAME AUTHOR 168

ABOUT THE ARTIST 172

ABOUT PŪNĀWAI PRESS 173

MAHALO

My thanks go out to the people that inspired the stories in *Beyond the Reef,* those that brought them to my attention, and those who made it a reality, especially Cheryl J. Kauha`a-Po, Charlotte Boteilho, Joseph Aspell, Amy Sirota, Laurel (Seeti) Douglass, Guy Gaumont, Virginia and David Sandell, Penny Davis, June Davis, Kalehua Darneal, Nancy Purdy, Keli`i Tau`a, Alaka`i Paleka, Keola Beamer, and Kī`ope Raymond.

Thanks to all that supported my previous effort, *Under Maui Skies and Other Stories.* Mahalo to those who helped with the promotion of that book, as well as those who housed, fed and chauffeured me in the Hawai`i, California and Nevada book tours: Father Jim Orsini and Pat Rickard, Saint Anthony High School (Wailuku), Barnes and Noble (Lahaina), Terry Waros, Kālele Bookstore and Divine Expressions (Kaunakakai, Moloka`i), Pat Banning, Bookends (Kailua, O`ahu), Native Books, Ward Warehouse (Honolulu, O`ahu), Barnes and Noble - The Pruneridge (San Jose, CA), Borders - Oak Ridge Mall (San Jose, CA), Deb, Dean and Devin Peyton, Vern Chang KKUP (Santa Clara, CA), Don Hedtke, Borders (Sacramento, CA), Michael Keene KVMR (Carson City, CA), Bookshop, West Portal Village (San Francisco, CA), Sedge Thompson of West Coast Live (San Francisco, CA), Book Sistas (Los Altos, CA), Half Price Books-Pacific Commons (Fremont, CA), Don Bradway KFOK (Georgetown, CA), Kaleolani DeSa and Lance Nagata, San Francisco Aloha Fest, Sandy Robinett World Music - KALW (San Francisco, CA), Borders (Union City, CA), Borders (Sand City, Monterey, CA), the people of Hercules, CA, Rodger and Georgia Bridgen and the folks of Henderson, Nevada, Robert and Miriam Chipp, Moana

Silva and her hālau, Steve Chipp, the folks of Colfax, Auburn and Sacramento, Dave Peyton, Chris and Theresa Keith, The National Writers Association - Honolulu Chapter, the MCC Peace Club and Chuck Carletta, Lacey and Emily Farm, *Ka Leo o Nā Koa*, Kaunoa Senior Center, The Administration of the University of Hawai`i - Maui College, Maui Literary Circle, Hawai`i Council of Portuguese Heritage, Cindy Paulos KAOI, Paul Wood, MANA`O Radio, Audrey Rocha Reed, Fred Guzman, Charlie Maxwell of the Pacific Radio Group, KNUI AM, Brickwood Galiteria, Skylark, *Nā `Ōiwi `Ōlino*, AM 940, Alaka`i Paleka, KPOA, Ollie and Val Dukelow, Kathy Beamer, Jacob Shafer, *Maui Time Weekly*, Margaret Seeto, *Honolulu Weekly*, Christine Thomas, *The Honolulu Advertiser*, Sky Barnhart, *Maui Weekly*, Liza Simon, *Ka Wai Ola*, Jeanne Cooper, *The San Francisco Chronicle*, Hawai`i Book Publishers Association, Tricia Eagar, Karlen Peterson, The Honolulu Book and Music Festival, M Denise C., Thomas Cummings, and John Holland.

Special Mahalo to Guy Gaumont for his time, effort and recording expertise.

Special thanks to all who voted to make *Under Maui Skies* the Nā Palapala Po`okela 2010 Readers' Choice Book of the Year.

Special thanks to Patrick Landeza, the gifted slack key artist, who I joyfully toured with during Summer 2010.

Of course I couldn't have done it without Arnold Kotler of Koa Books.

PRONOUNCING HAWAIIAN WORDS

The Hawaiian alphabet consists of twelve letters—five vowels and seven consonants. The vowels are pronounced similarly to Latin, Spanish, Italian, and Japanese, except the letter "e," which is pronounced like the e in get. Hawaiian consonants are similar to those in English, but have less aspiration. Under certain circumstances, (after i and e, and optionally after a or as the initial letter), the letter is pronounced as a soft v.

Generally, the accent of words is on the second-to-last syllable. The ʻokina, or glottal stop—it looks like a "left apostrophe" between certain vowels—is a quick stopping of the flow of air, causing each of the vowels to be enunciated separately. The kahako, or macron—a line placed over a vowel—indicates that the syllable should be held for approximately two beats, rather than one. When pronouncing certain diphthongs (ei, cu, oi, ou, ai, ae, ao, au), emphasize the first vowel, and then roll into the second.

PREFACE

In *Under Maui Skies and Other Stories*, I wrote seven tales of the Valley Isle all in different genres, different Maui locations, and different time periods. The evolutionary step was obvious. Like my own early life, the first stories were immediately based on Maui. Now they take place in settings not only on Maui but—*Beyond the Reef*.

This second collection of stories includes some specifically Maui based tales like *The Big L, I Walked with the Night Marchers*, and *The Teenage Creature from the Black Lagoon*. But, like my later life, the new stories take the reader from beyond the Valley Isle to the far corners of the Earth. However, no matter if the story is set on a neighbor island, the mainland, or even Europe, you'll find Maui roots still there: Liliu‘okalani returning from ‘Ulupalakua's Rose Ranch in *A Day at the Palace/A Night at the Opera*, Father Damien in *The Fires of Pu‘uoumi* volunteering for Kalaupapa at St. Anthony's in Wailuku, Ikua Purdy, one of Hawaii's greatest paniolo, remembered at his Kula gravesite in *The Trail to Mānā*, and Ha‘alilio and Kamehameha III in Lahaina planning their quest for sovereignty in *For the Rose of the Chiefs*.

In addition to some of the genre employed in *Under Maui Skies* like the ghost story, there's a sampling here of other genres—the crime caper, a coming of age tale, a sports (surf) yarn and an inspirational story, some set in new Maui locations and time periods.

There's also a new collection of *kaona* in this edition, the majority dedicated to the male members of my family. Because *kaona* are metaphoric, (individuals are represented by something in nature), it was only natural that some of my fishermen uncles would be best represented by fish.

This book is dedicated to Paulette and Joe Medeiros for their
unwavering support of my personal as well as artistic efforts,
even from small kid time.

I WALKED WITH THE NIGHT MARCHERS
Ua Hele Au me Nā Huaka'i Pō

He was called "*haole* boy". After all, he had typical white traits—blonde hair and blue eyes. Only after hearing him break into pidgin, or when he let the *'ōlelo Hawai'i* flow as smooth as Moloka'i honey, did new acquaintances realize that they had not run into a seasonal windsurfer at Ho'okipa.

Maka Polū had been born and raised in Wailuku by his Hawaiian mother in Mill Camp, just behind St. Anthony's. His father had long hightailed it back to Pinckneyville, Illinois—he couldn't stand Maui's humidity, his wife grateful when he actually left; she said she couldn't stand a sweat hog, anyway. She had long replaced Maka Polu's last name—Bannon—with Pu'ali—her maiden name. Paul had, over time, been rechristened "Maka Polū", like the swimming pool game, by his brown-eyed schoolyard friends. Maka Polū gradually grew into the name; it was readily accepted when he noticed that high school girls were attracted to his baby blues.

Scholarships failed to come near graduation. Maka Polū was a bit disappointed that he had not yet gotten away to experience the Mainland, but his love of the Hawaiian language and culture was the magnet that held him in the islands. His mother had always insisted that he be trilingual—fluent in English, Pidgin, and Hawaiian. When Hawaiian language immersion schools blossomed, he was encouraged by his mother to enroll.

He was now at Maui College engaged in his native language, steadily moving toward fluency. His previous easily distracted, undisciplined high school environment was replaced by stimulating classes wrapped in the stories, culture, and language of Hawai`i.

He was as typical as any college student. He loved to chase girls, party, and "hang" with his friends. His closest buddies, Kimo and Ryan, were always up for a few kicks on Maui before they would eventually transfer to UH, Mānoa or UH, Hilo. Diving, camping, and fishing were par for the course. However, their love with midnight tennis would drive them to a new experience that would change their lives forever.

Midnight tennis had followed midnight basketball. The usual agenda was to get in an early nap, set the alarm clock just before midnight, and head out to outdoor basketball and tennis courts. The game was officially sanctioned by at least one "brewski" prior to the toss up or serve, followed by several others after the winning score. By the fourth or fifth month of those after-dark sports, the boys were in search of other athletic endeavors.

Kimo was the first to suggest midnight golf one morning while gorging himself on pancakes at Tasty Crust. Ryan resisted by insisting that sneaking into a private golf course wouldn't be as easy as gaining access to a county b-ball or tennis court. The lights at the county facilities stayed on all night to accommodate the likes of all-hour workers getting in their exercise for the day.

Maka Polū had reservations about the new venture. "Plus,

those golf courses all have security. It's gonna be tough."

"Maybe not so tough," added Kimo with the backup plan. "My aunty works at the Waikapū Golf Course restaurant. I went to pick her up late one night. She was the last one out. Security locked the main gate after Aunty came through, then he headed to other checkpoints. She mentioned that the main buildings had electronic devices, so I guess as long as we stay away from those, there should be no problem."

"We can use flashlights, turn them on for the swing or the putt, then turn them off, and on to the next hole," proposed Ryan.

"A bright night is definitely out of the question. Gotta have no moon, gotta be the darkest night," insisted Maka. Each raised their last bites of hotcakes and toasted, their forks clicking, "To Midnight Golf!"

The boys used their stealth modes of transportation to get to the golf course on the fourteenth of the month—the moon in *Hoaka*. Maka had learned that *Hoaka* had another meaning besides "crescent". It also meant spirit or ghost. It was on this night when the ʻuhane cast shadows and frightened even the fish in the sea.

It was close to 10:00 p.m. when they reached their destination and hid their bikes in the bougainvillea thicket just off the road. Crickets were the only performers of a doleful mantra in a darkness that could bite. The boys were nonetheless satisfied. This moonless night meant great cover. Feeling more secure in nature's black camouflage, they trudged their way up along one of the weedy breaks between parcels of cane field; an eerie, whispered rustling replaced the mournful chatter of insects. Luckily, a steady two-day rain had ceased. The conditions for midnight golf seemed perfect. They waited on a bluff at the edge of towering cane stalks to witness the parade of employees' cars winding down to the exit gate, the laborers ending their day. The three students, of course, were waiting for the approach of the guard in the small, white security truck who would secure the lock at the main gate down near the highway. Finally, the lights from his Mazda passed them; the driver hopped out, fulfilled his duties, and disappeared into the night, leaving the boys alone in shadow.

"He should be gone till his 3 a.m. check. We'll be home and asleep by then," Ryan reassured the others.

"Okay, let's go."

As they proceeded up the hill, Kimo suggested playing only two holes, the twelfth and thirteenth. "They're the farthest from any course building."

The quiet, too eerie moments of silence between conversations bred small samples of paranoia as they trudged up the hill. Unuttered thoughts raced in circles in their brains like a not so merry-go-round. "What if security returns?" "What was that sound?" "What kind of foul play…?"

Finally, they reached their destination. The butterflies that fluttered in their stomachs were calmed temporarily by the awe of Kahului's distant lights and the commanding view of Haleakalā, barely lit by the streaming stars.

"I'll go first," insisted Maka.

"Not until our initiation ceremony," announced Kimo as he pulled three Miller Lights from his backpack.

"My *mahalo* to the bartender. It's still cold," said Maka.

Ryan held his Miller high. "The Three Mousketeers!"

"All for one and one for…" he paused.

"Britney!" they toasted, in homage to the second most famous Mousketeer, next to Annette.

Maka moved into position. "The added challenge to this game is to find the ball once we've hit it, so we'll have to try extra hard to get it near the green."

"Lowest score after six holes?" asked Ryan. The other two agreed as Maka drove the ball. After the other two took their swings, the trio headed down the hill to find their marked balls. However, even their flashlights were of no use; all the balls had obviously landed in the thick lantana. Ryan, tired of poking around in the high grass and getting scratched by unfriendly shrub, finally called for a game change.

"We'll just putt from of the edge of green #13." The others agreed wholeheartedly.

As they approached the green, all three were taken aback by the severe quiet of the farthest hole—#13. Some of the shadows of the surrounding shrubs seemed to whisper senseless talk when brushed by the wind racing down Ka'onohua Gulch. Maka Polū had learned about this rarely studied area for a paper in his Hawaiian culture class. A seemingly lifeless landscape to most, these ruffled ravines had a dramatic past of war and carnage.

"I'll go first again," insisted Maka. Kimo pointed his flashlight in a straight line from the ball at the edge of the green to the hole. Maka tapped the ball toward the *puka*; it swirled around the lip once and continued a few feet from the hole. "Arggghhhh," Maka moaned in disgust. He resisted defeat, concentrated on his second effort, and led the ball in.

Suddenly, a cold wind raced out of nowhere and put a shiver in all three spines. Kimo, about to place his ball on the lip of the green, suddenly stopped.

"What's the matter, Kimo?" asked Ryan

"I dunno. I… I… I think I hear drums."

Ryan taunted his buddy. "Yeah, right. In fact, the *Menehune* are holding a dance over in the next gulch." The rolling sound of thunder bowled south from the Big Island. "See. That's your drums, some leftover storm clouds from the last two days."

Maka ignored the scientific plausibility and reiterated Kimo's comment. "No, Ryan. He's not lying. I think I heard it too!"

Ryan did a 360, in case someone with drum in hand was lurking behind them. "You guys! Oh, no! Look!"

There, in the distance, two lights pierced the darkness. It was the security guard's truck.

"You think he saw our flashlight?!"

"I don't think so! What's he doing back here?" added Maka.

"If he's headed this way, then we'll worry," said Ryan.

The truck confirmed Ryan's worry. It was heading up the hill and onto the golfcart path that directly lead up to hole #13.

"Quick! Duck down in the brush!" The boys climbed down the lip of elevated hole #13 and slid into the muddy gully just below it, their eyes peering through the shadowed bushes.

Kimo whispered, "Do you think he saw us?"

Ryan whispered back, "Tonight, of all nights, he chooses not to follow his routine."

The security guard brought the vehicle to a soft stop, walked over to the small rail that corralled the farthest hole, took out a cigarette and smoked it, while taking in the stars flickering above Haleakalā. It was now obvious to the boys that it was one of his smoke stops and eventually relieved as the interrupter stomped out the butt, jumped into the truck, and drove off.

The relief was altered when all three again heard a *pahu* in the distance. They turned their heads. Suddenly, on a small footpath that ran along the bottom edge of Pu'u Moe Gulch, they saw a torch, then a second.

Ryan's *'opihi* eyes spoke with faux laughter, "They must be some actors. They shooting a movie down there!"

"Like hell. It's *Huaka'i Pō*!" said Maka Polū, dazed.

"What the hell is *hui, huwe...*?" questioned Ryan.

"*Huaka'i Pō*, Ryan, Night Marchers, *lōlō*," translated Kimo. "Let's get the hell out of here. Whatever! I no like face Night Marchers, or one psychotic acting troupe."

All three realized how easy it had been to slide down the ravine but more difficult to get solid footing on the soaked red dirt. Ryan made an end run along an easier path back up and onto the thirteenth green. As he bee-lined, he uttered, in *sotto voce*, a final plan, "Everyone for themselves. Meet down at the bikes!" He blended into the dark night with Kimo at his tail.

Maka was tugged by the fright and fascination at the sight of the *Huaka'i Pō*. He knew from tradition that a look at or from one of them would result in death. He wanted to witness such a phenomenon, but his better sense prevailed; he thought he'd be able to claw his way up the slippery gulch. After a few attempts, he finally thought he had it. He grabbed a large rock for an anchor.

"Oh, no!" Maka whined as he heard the soil around the boulder crumble; the stone fell back and both rolled uncontrollably down into the gully. As he tumbled, Maka's tee shirt was snagged by a weathered fallen tree branch, ripped from his body, and left behind like a shredded ghost fluttering in the wind. Each attempt to stop was even more treacherous than the previous. Maka went head over heels until he slammed into a stopped-up bog filled with goop from the days of rain that had doused the usually dry ravines.

When he opened his eyes, he noticed that his now half-naked body was lying under a small bridge composed of strapped *hau* boughs, a section along the trail of the oncoming spirits.

He hoped that his now blackened body was enough of a camouflage. He reminded himself again that, traditionally, no one was to look at Night Marchers, but his curiosity was now more compelling than protocol and prudence.

Through the slats of the creaking *hau* bridge, he counted as they crossed: a torchbearer, a drummer, two males, two females, and a second torchbearer. One male was missing from what Maka had learned in his Hawaiian culture class.

Maka Polū held his breath like he had not held it before. As the final torchbearer crossed, Maka thought that the worst had passed. He was wrong.

"*E Kūlia!*" the leader commanded, his voice somewhat distorted. "*Hele lālani!*" He thrust the torch down into Maka Polu's hiding place. Maka thought that his hour had come, but also knew that the command was to get into formation, to get in the line. The college student was confused. Didn't the leader know that Maka was from among the living? "*Hele lālani!*" commanded the man with the torch.

Maka climbed out of the small bog, his khaki Burmies and body dripping with the mud he had been squatting in. He succumbed, feeling that if he refused, death might be the result. He climbed onto the crude bridge and into formation ahead of the torchbearer.

"*Naue i mua!*" The group continued their journey with the forward march command.

Maka, in a dazed state, to say the least, made some observations as they sloughed along the trail. Most of what he saw coincided with tales of the few who had encountered and miraculously survived Night Marchers.

The two men, two women, drummer and two torchbearers he believed to be a *paukū*—the equivalent of a military squad. But there were supposed to be three men. The torchbearer had obviously thought that Maka Polū was the missing warrior when he coaxed him out of the ditch.

All the actions of the fighting lost squad seemed programmed, with no honest expression. Even the *oli* they chanted along the trail was listless, like a child forced to memorize his times tables. No glow of life projected from their eyes. At the thought of eyes, the college student grew paranoid, wondering if these walking dead had noticed his glimmer of life, much less his baby blues. He felt slightly secure that the inky ooze that still dripped from his head was cover for any hint of his state.

The sing-song chant they murmured as they marched told who they were. They were the warriors of Kalaniopu'u of the Big Island. They were on their way to battle the men and women of Kahekili—to take over control of Maui. They were ignorant of its outcome, convinced this was the 1700s.

The first of the five called out that Waikapū was ahead. This squad had fallen behind the *pakaliona* for some reason. A battalion scout had, earlier, brought back news to the delayed squad that the whole Hawai'i battalion would attack an encampment of Kahekili's Maui forces in the sand dunes just north of Waikapū.

"*Kūlia! Maha!*" yelled out the commander as they approached a glade of Hawaiian plum trees and *kukui*. He told them they would rest for an hour's equivalent, prepare their weapons, and attack Kahekili's defenders on the dunes of the 'Ōma'oma'o Plain.

Like robots, Kalaniopuu's attackers checked their weapons—oblivious to the fellow former humans that sat beside them. They mindlessly sharpened the spear tips and wooden *koa* blades that they would plunge into the hearts of the Maui *koa*.

Upon completion, they swigged *wai* in small gourds which they had dipped into a nearby streamlet. They ate unconsciously. They didn't sound the "haaa" of living thirsty men or the smacking lips of humans as they nibbled dried ʻ*ulu* and potato. A few minutes later, some began a rote game of *kōnane*—it never evolved into a game of wisecracks, laughs, heated competition, or camaraderie like players of the Earth.

After some time, the *alakaʻi* checked the sharpness of his shark tooth weapon by slicing his finger. Black, not red, dust-like pus coagulated. The leader roused the men like he had performed this play a thousand times and summoned them to battle, "*E hele, e kākou!*" The men and women gathered together to make their final trek to "victory". They moved out of the lush vegetation around Waikapū, across Piʻilani's dirt road, and onto the sand dunes. According to the last message from the preceding units, they presumed the battle was just over the next major bluff.

Maka Polū knew that these walking dead must engage soon and return to the netherworld from which they came before the sun cast its rays over Haleakalā. After some time, they finally reached their destination and climbed the steep incline. They were confused, however, as they ascended because they heard no sounds of battle, no wailing from victims being sliced by daggers or spears in their backs, chests, and throats. They then knew why. There was no one there, only a vast plain of thick white sand illuminated weakly by the stars. The leader stopped and surmised, "*Mamao iki aku paha.*" His command, that the battle was farther away, was followed by his insistence from *kahuna* that they stay on the well trodden path that ran across the thick sinking, seemingly endless dunes.

As Maka Polū moved on with the squad, a sense of *déjà vu* came over him. He had seen or rather read about this battle before. As the *kahuna* had predicted, when all the members of the squad had traversed most of the sand, they would be suddenly surprised as Kahekili's warriors, men and women alike, exploded from the ground. They would cast aside the *kapa* that covered them and the reeds that allowed them to breathe while they lay buried in the evening sands. They waited patiently until Kalaniopuu's *koa* were deep in their net, then the sluices at both ends were slammed shut.

Maka Polū wanted to warn them, but his precognition would put his own life into jeopardy. He was prepared to run at the first call of battle. Suddenly, the battle squad went into shock, then violence. They poked their weapons at the air, slashed their knives at nothingness. They grunted, groaned, and sweated, embattled with the unseen. They grabbed at their already existing scars inflicted from their confused response to the surprise attack. Maka Polū was awed at first by the battle against invisible people. Bathed in the excitement of that moment, he thought he was secure, merely a curious bystander to history. The notion was quickly dispelled when he saw, unlike the Night Marchers, a Maui warrior lunge toward him. It seemed that Maka was the only one that actually saw his enemy. The combatant leaped toward him, and Maka Polu's instinct of survival kicked in. He grabbed the *koa*'s neck, but the warrior was too skilled for a college boy's hold. Kahekili's warrior lifted Maka Polū into the air and slammed him down upon his knee; the young man lost consciousness.

When Maka Polū finally awoke, he surveyed the scene with squinted eyes, afraid that if an enemy warrior saw him alive, those *koa* would finish him off. Luckily, he saw none of Kahekili's soldiers; what came into focus were the soft sand mounds now littered with seven scattered bodies.

Maka Polū raised himself and dusted the sand off the caked

muck that covered his body. At that point, the contemporary witness froze in hideous awe. Kalaniopuu's warriors raised themselves from the dead as if nothing had happened and went into formation with the intent to return to where they came from. They prepared to retrace the trail they had traveled on. How Maka Polū wanted to talk to the others but, in fear, remained silent. Still dazed from the battle and the resurrections, he would be quiet with the intent to escape back to the living once he reached the small bridge near the golf course. He would make up some excuse, tell the marchers that he'd eventually catch up, then run to the safety of Ryan and Kimo, who he was sure would be searching for him.

The defeated *koa* trudged on limply, exhausted. Maka thought. How many times had they done this? They retraced their steps across Pi'ilani's road, onto the trail that ran above and beyond Waikapū, and past the golf course.

As they approached the green where he had last left his friends, Maka noticed flashlights in the distance. But they were nowhere near the little *hau* bridge. The search party was way up the gulch. They would be too far to see him as they scoured the untamed ravines far up the mountain. His heart suddenly welled up. It was Kimo and Ryan near the thirteenth hole! He was happy they had returned. He could hear them shouting his name; "Maka, Maka, Maka! Maka Polū" echoed across the valley. He tried to shout back but nothing came from his throat. He grabbed at it, and shuddered. It was only then that he felt the buildup of scar tissue around his neck.

Maka attempted to return, but his legs were not under his own control; it had been ordained that he continue the journey back to Ma'alae'a. The flashlights of Kimo and Ryan were turned just in time for Maka's friends to see the flicker from the Night Marcher's torch as it disappeared behind the ridge of the next valley. The two students looked at each other and thought they saw the final glint of the *maka polū* of their friend. The dead man turned his head. The searching flashlights slowly faded in the distance like his faded hope of ever returning to walk among the living.

A DAY AT THE PALACE / A NIGHT AT THE OPERA

He Lā i Ka Hale Aliʻi / He Pō i Ke Keaka Mele

Liliuʻokalani was crouched, her knees tight against her chest, in the window seat of the Music Room at the palace. The future queen, addressed by her baptismal name, Lydia, among family and friends, was hoping for an inspirational breakthrough considering all the doodling she had inflicted on her tablet. Where were those muses? Even her retreat to the soothing Rose Ranch at ʻUlupalakua had yielded no opera. The topsy-turvy return ride across the Molokaʻi Channel from Maui on the *Kinaʻu* the previous day had, perhaps, distracted her, along with her husband's mischief. But even with a new day, nothing was coming. She knew that she had lots of material just from the shenanigans of her Kamehameha clan, but the format—that was the stickler. Her mind was additionally side tracked by the noisy bevy of wagons that came and went to and from the palace along King Street. Her brother, David, had left that morning on his round-the-world tour. She would be acting monarch in his absence and receive all the exotic furniture and artifacts that he'd send back to Hawai`i as he visited those faraway lands. `Iolani Palace would be officially dedicated when brother David returned; for the next number of months, life at the royal residence would be as chaotic as Chinatown and its congregation of Saturday customers.

The quiet of the gold room was disturbed by the clip-clop of boots ascending the staircase. "Excuse me, ma`am," said one of the two burly men that sauntered in through the large doors. "Is you the one in charge here?"

The future queen played along. "You might say that I'm the palace interior decorator."

"Then you's the one. We got here a billiard table for the king."

"You'll have to lug it upstairs, across the hall," responded the princess.

The two men looked at each other with grimaced faces of pain that they'd be feeling shortly when they hefted the lead laden table up to the second story.

Lydia resettled herself in the window seat, hoping that the plot line of the opera would finally materialize. She had been bitten by the opera bug since she was twenty. Her baptism was Donizetti's *Daughter of the Regiment*, the first legitimate opera to play Honolulu at the Varieties Theater. Perhaps her opera would be inspired by her favorite Donizetti work: *Lucia di Lammermore*. She loved the melancholic story but, on second thought, believed that Honolulu audiences would feel the subject matter too weighty or bizarre for simple, carefree Hawai`i. After all, opera audiences of 1881 were the same that attended boxing matches and sword swallowing. She had definitely heard David's litany of complaints by producers who objected to police presence at productions of *Norma* and *The*

Barber of Seville.

One thing she had definitely accomplished was her choice of pen name. She had noted that all the female opera singers that had visited town had preceded their names with "Madam" like the sopranos, Avalos and Austin. She had scrawled her pseudonym, Madam Aorena, just below her listless working title, *An Opera*.

The peace of the palace was broken by the hearty laughter of Bernice and Miriam. They charged into the room, sheet music fluttering to the ground.

Lydia looked up quizzically. "Here so soon?"

"Cousin," Bernice Bishop insisted, "with all this luxury, David must have at least one clock in the palace? Didn't you tell us to come by 11:00?"

Lydia ran over to the clock on the mantel. "Oh, my God. It's eleven?! Oh, Lord, where did the time fly? We're having lunch with… I've got to run downstairs to the kitchen and make sure everything's ready. We're having… "

"Slow down, sister. No need to run all the way down there. Use the new invention. Oh, and by the way, so good to see you, cousin," offered Miriam Likelike, the Governess of O`ahu. The three young women kissed each other.

"Good idea," said Lydia. She bee-lined for the phone in the corner. Still not used to the new invention, Lydia spoke loudly into the long black horn attached to a polished oak box, "Hello, hello, Tessie?" A shriek blared through the telephone and rebounded throughout the palace.

"Oh, I'm sorry, Tessie. I didn't mean to scare you."

"They're gonna have to blow a whistle, ring a bell, or whack a gong, so we won't be startled by sudden voices," insisted the cook.

"I know, Tessie," the acting queen said. "And we're speaking awfully loud. There's a tendency to belt it out like we were far away in Timbuktu. I guess we'll just have to get used to Mr. Bell's toy. By the way, how is the luncheon coming?"

"I'm afraid we'll have to forgo the cake I ordered for dessert," apologized the cook.

"What? Why no cake?" she queried.

"It had to do with all that ruckus and the fire bells you heard last night."

"I didn't hear anything. I was four sheets to the wind. I think that the rough boat trip back from Maui did me in. So what happened?"

"The Celestial Bakery caught fire last night."

"Again?" laughed Liliu`okalani. "Well, how about… fruit… that's a healthy substitute." The cook agreed, and Lydia returned to her sisters. "Tessie said that the Celestial Bakery caught fire last night. Sorry, no sweets today."

"Again?" chuckled Bernice.

"That was my same reaction, Pauahi," added Lydia.

Miriam snickered nostalgically. "Remember that sign in the Celestial Bakery window that we memorized as school kids? Now, how did that go?"

Bernice cued the others and they all joined in…

> "Good people all…
> walk in and buy
> of Sam and Moe
> good cake and pie
> bread hard and soft
> for land and sea
> Celestial made
> come buy of we."

Miriam got back to the subject. "Ah, seems only yesterday when we could eat with abandon. I'll gladly forgo dessert."

Bernice reendorsed Miriam in her hoity toity voice. "Indeed. We must keep our figyahs svelte for the theeaatah."

"In fact, I don't know if I could eat anything, anyway," added Miriam.

Lydia insisted, "Well, I wish that you at least nibble because I've invited Henri Berger over to the palace for lunch—you know, a little *mahalo* for his work with the Honolulu Amateur Dramatic Club, particularly for producing *H.M.S. Pinafore* in the islands. I give it to him; he's gutsy doing the work of unknown writers like this Gilbert and Sullivan."

Miriam countered the doubt. "Cousin, it's a great show! You'll be quite pleased."

"So, you two thespians excited about tonight?" asked Lydia.

"Oh, Lord. We're only in the chorus but my stomach's a-fluttering, and the show's just hours away," moaned Bernice, Lydia's cousin and old classmate at the Royal School.

Miriam continued. "It's not like those highfulutin operas. It's funny. I especially like the… "

Lydia stopped her. "Miriam! You always do that—reveal the ending of books and spoil them. Don't tell me. I want to be surprised. Anyway," continued the future queen, "you came to use the piano to practice for tonight, so don't let me stop you." Lydia resettled herself in the window box with its soft cushions and made another attempt at Hawaii's first opera.

Bernice and Miriam headed over to the grand piano, set up the sheet music and pounded out the introduction. The cousins warbled:

For I'm called Little Buttercup—dear Little Buttercup,

Though I can never tell why,
But still I'm called Buttercup—poor little Buttercup
Sweet Little Buttercup I!

There was a loud crash in the foyer. The two amateur artists stopped their singing. "What was that?!" brayed Miriam.

The two burly movers framed themselves at the Music Room door.

"Sorry to bother you, madam inferior decorator, ladies, but we gonna need more help lugging that two-ton son-of-a… oh, pardon, misses, billiard table upstairs. It's as heavy as hell… Oh pardon, ma`am."

Once again Liliuokalani rose from her non-inspirational position.

"I'll call a couple of the male help to give you a hand." She lifted the receiver. "Hello? Mr. Santos! Hello? Oh, sorry, Mr. Santos. Mr. Santos? I didn't mean… Are you okay? Just take a couple of breaths. Oh, Mr. Santos, I really didn't mean to scare you. I know it's loud. They're going to have to turn it down. No, no one's dead. We just need a little help getting the billiard table upstairs. Can you grab Manolo and come over to the Music Room?"

Bernice and Miriam continued.

I've snuff and tobaccy, and excellent jacky,
I've scissors and watches and knives
I've ribbons and laces to set off the faces
Of pretty young sweethearts and wives.

I've treacle and toffee, I've tea and I've coffee
Soft tommy and succulent chops
I've chickens and conies and pretty polonies

and excellent peppermint drops.

Mr. Santos and Manolo finally appeared at the door, but silenced by the two movers, their palms in the wait mode. The four men bobbed their heads in rhythm, attempting the final chorus.

Then buy of your Buttercup—dear Little Buttercup
Sailors should never be shy
So, buy of your Buttercup—poor Little Buttercup
Come of your Buttercup buy!

The audience of manual laborers applauded the singing sisters.

"The chorus thanks you. Now off to that billiard table," urged the acting inferior decorator. In attempted unison, the movers sang *Goodnight, Ladies* and left with the palace muscle.

Lydia had been surprised by the words of *H.M.S. Pinafore*. "Fascinating—these lyrics," she mused out loud.

Bernice retorted, "Well, it ain't Faust; that's for sure." Miriam turned the page, and the cousins continued their practice.

Lydia had not made it halfway across the teakwood floor, back toward her tablet, when she heard her full name, "*Lili'u Loloku Walania Wewehi Kahaka'eha!*" It was Henri Berger. His voice reverberated from the first floor up to the ceiling's koa molding.

"Henri, I'm glad you made it. I know it's a busy day for you."

Scanning the renovated building, Henri quipped, "Now we don't have to go to New York to play the Palace." The two friends hugged and kissed. Henri turned his attention to Bernice and Miriam. "And how are my finest songbirds?"

Suddenly, a loud scream penetrated the palace. It came from across the hall. Lydia and her guests raced to the source of the murder, only to find Mr. Santos, Manolo, and the two movers caught up in a frenzied dance.

"What's the matter, Mr. Santos?" yelled out the future queen.

"A large rat jumped out from under the table." The periphery of all the eyes in the room caught the shadow that dashed behind the upright piano and spittoon. "There!" yelled the chorus of exterminators.

One of the burley movers insisted, "It looked like a rat but… I… dunno… "

In the midst of the debate, the mystery rodent bolted through the long skirts of Miriam and Bernice. The chorus girls let out piercing shrieks before they were parted again, this time by the sweaty men in pursuit of the wayward critter, Manolo taking up the rear while reassuring the Crown Regent, "Not to worry, we catch heem." The rumbling thunder rolled down the grand staircase until all was quiet, everyone assured that the uninvited tourist had exited the building. The cautious ladies and a somewhat bewildered Berger returned to the Music Room.

"Now, where were we? Oh, yes. Good morning, Henri… " started Bernice.

"Or is it the Captain of the *Pinafore*?" finished Miriam. "Are you as excited as we are?"

"As exited as a rodent on the run," quipped Henri, as the jittery females rechecked the doorway. "I know we have a good show and, thanks to two lovely ladies, we have a company I have confidence in. The audiences will be quite surprised… and so will you, Lydia."

"Well, lunch is almost ready, Henri," responded his musical

collaborator, "ah, except for the dessert. You might say it was overcooked at the Celestial Bakery last night."

"I heard. Listen, I'll be happy with one of those new Hayden mangoes from Mr. Ching Chock's experimental garden down the road."

Miriam and Bernice retreated to the piano, this time with Maestro Berger assisting. No sooner had they gotten into rehearsal when they were startled by a loud "Hello!" that reverberated across the room. It was Mr. Bell's contraption. All three of the rehearsers turned to give stink eye to the new, noisy housemate. Temporarily believing that the Music Room was possessed, Lydia too responded to the wall demon, wondering if she would ever get used to the interruptive invention… "Hello?"

A nasally imitator announced. "Ship to shore for Crown Princess Liliu`okalani!"

Lydia could hear the background of banging kitchenware. "Tessie, stop playing around!"

"Do I really sound like Tessie?" said the now natural voice.

"David?! What in the world… ? Where are you?"

"Sister, `Iolani Palace is the only place with phones, yet. Soon we will be able to talk from boat to palace, but now I'm calling from the kitchen."

She relayed to Henri, "It's David!"

"I thought he left on his round the world trip?" uttered Henri.

"David, what are you doing here?" she bellowed back.

"There was a small fire in the galley as we were about to depart. Lots of the food staples ended up precooked including all our flour and rice. We wouldn't be able to make it to San Francisco without those basic provisions, so I'm back here until they restock the galley. I didn't want to bother you; we were going to pick up something to eat, then head back down to the waterfront."

Suddenly, Lydia heard a racket in the background. She heard David yell, "Manolo, what the he…?" Pots crashed, pans clanged and banged. Shrieks of "Seize him! Stop him!" peeled in the background. Finally, David returned to the phone and issued a large sigh. "Sorry, Lydia, Mr. Santos, Manolo and two strangers came barging through the kitchen. I…?"

"An unidentified critter is visiting the palace," stated Lydia. "Henri, Miriam, and Bernice are also here, and we're just about to head down to the dining room for lunch. Come and join us."

"I think I can sweet talk Tessie into a couple of new settings, because guess who's here with me? It's Annis."

Liliu`okalani got exited; she eyeballed Henri. "Annis?"

"Yes, her ship pulled in from Australia while we were postponing our departure."

"Well, tell Hawaii's prima donna that she is expected at lunch as well. See you in the dining room."

Lydia called at the sisters who were belting out, *"He's the Captain of the Pinafore."*

"Henri, Bernice, Miriam, David's here! The ship has been delayed. He's here with Annis Montague, who just got in. We're all meeting in the dining room. Let's go!" The women were excited to see the daughter of the missionary couple that had educated the Kamehameha clan at the Royal School.

As the entourage descended the stairs, Henry asked the future queen, "So, how was your trip to Maui?"

"Oh, I stayed up at the Rose Ranch in `Ulupalakua. So relaxing. You might call the inhalation of eucalyptus, camphor and pine a kind of aroma therapy," replied Liliuokalani.

"Was your husband up at the ranch with you?"

"Well, it was relaxing until John finally showed up, claiming that being Governor of Maui has many demands." Lydia lowered her voice, "But, according to the gossip, not busy enough to be a ladies' man. Oh, I warned Mr. Dominis in no uncertain terms that it would be his *kuleana* and not mine if a little *keiki* should pop up along the line."

Henri changed the subject to share some good news with Liliuʻokalani. "Oh, by the way, I got an invitation by the Knights Templar to introduce *Aloha ʻOe* at their triennial conclave in San Francisco in '83. I hope the lyricist can join me for the event. And perhaps, Lydia, while we're in The City, we could find a publisher; maybe Pacific Music might take it on."

"I'd love to, Henri, if there are no other conflicts," said the princess.

The group fluttered into the State Dining Room to greet David and Annis.

"I don't think brother wants to leave home," teased Lydia, as everyone shared their Aloha. "Annis, taking a break after your Australian tour?"

Hawaii's first bona fide opera star said, "Yes. I'm here to see the family, but I'm offering my talents to fund the Little Church of Waikīkī and Henri's Honolulu Amateur Musical Society and Dramatic Club." Everyone clapped and offered their thanks.

"And we'll gladly accept," added David. "Now, take a seat, everyone. I hate to eat and run… the world awaits."

Tessie and the servants came and went with the fish and poi meal, and the group settled into a variety of topics, dominated this day by the world of opera. As they awaited their dessert, Lydia queried Annis about Juliette and Amos Cooke. "Have your parents finally accepted your career now that you've been acclaimed? You know, everyone's still talking about your achievement with Hayden's *Creation* the last time you came to town."

"Oh, thank you, Lydia. Father doesn't say much. But you know mother by now, pig headed, as usual. Oh, she'll come to the concerts, but I can hear that skirt rustling in the audience, Mother squirming in her seat through the whole performance. She still can't believe a Cooke with her Montague namesake is prancing on the stage, or what she calls—the Devil's Workshop."

Tessie finally presented the dessert of golden mangoes and succulent lychee.

"Tessie, you read my mind. From Mr. Chock's experimental garden?" asked Henri.

"Indeed. You know, we'll have to plant some of these on the grounds," replied the cook. Oohs and aahs followed each slurp of the new fruit.

Henri lapped up the fruit and saluted it, "These are indeed heavenly gifts! Burnt offerings! Food for the gods! Mōhailani!"

As Lydia digested Henri's inspiration, and the succulent citrus, a tornado suddenly hit the room without warning, rising to a crescendo of shouts and screams. As Tessie turned, she was bounced around like a deflating balloon, nearly escaping being trampled by the palace help and the billiard table movers, this time carrying varied implements of capture.

"Get him!" The furry creature did a scurried loop of the room. "Stop the weasel!" another yelled. The diners, in shock, responded by rising, the ladies up on the chairs, skirts raised.

"That's no weasel; it's a mongoose!" insisted David.

"We don't have mongoose in Hawai`i," countered Lydia.

"We obviously have one," declared the king.

The mongoose hunters raced out of the room after the little

monster. A new face in work clothes appeared at the dining room door. He apologized, "Sorry, your majesty. He bore his way through the cage."

"Everyone," said David, "let me introduce to you Mr. Sabbatini, from the experimental station across the street. The Hawai`i Planters are considering introducing the mongoose to get rid of the rats that are plaguing the cane fields."

Mr. Sabbatini apologized profusely and, after insisting the escapee would be captured, left the room. Everyone descended the chairs and finished their bowls of mango and lychee.

"I hate to leave all of you now, but I have a world to sail around," said King David Kalākaua, pulling his chair back. I wish all of you success with the *H.M.S. Pinafore* tonight. Aloha."

"Bon voyage… for real, brother," wished Lydia as she kissed him.

The rest gave their best wishes and David returned to his ship, *The City of Sydney*.

"Well, we'd all better get going too," said Henri. "We've got a show to do. See you after at the reception, Lydia. And *mahalo* for lunch."

"The same," said Miriam.

"Break a leg, sisters," wished Lydia, as she escorted them to the door.

"Oh, Annis, with the king out of town, why don't you join me in the Royal Box at the Music Hall tonight? Maybe you could give me some hints on my new opera."

"I'd love that. Thank you!" replied Annis. "Shall I call for you at 6:00 p.m.?"

"Perfect," said Lydia. "Then, we'll stroll across the street."

As she wished aloha to the group, Lydia noticed, in the distance, an embarrassed Mr. Sabbatini, with cage in hand, returning the loose mongoose to his place of residence. The palace would now be finally quiet for the rest of the day.

Lydia sat in the Royal Box with Annis that night, exhausted by the hectic day, but mesmerized by the world of Gilbert and Sullivan. Finally, on this night, she had found a form for her opera. It wouldn't be the heavy operas of Europe like *Il Travatore* and *Faust*. Instead, it would be about the joyful aloha of living in Paradise. She would poke fun at the court intrigues of her brothers and sisters and herself with the playful operetta in the style of the British composer and his lyricist brother.

The muse had finally appeared. Mōhailani sat between Liliuokalani and Annis.

THE FIRES OF PU`UO`UMI
Nā Ahi o Pu`uo`umi

Damien felt a renewed sense of loneliness as he watched Father Evard fade into the twilight. What in the world had he agreed to? He debated the fine line between service for God and insanity. Hadn't the Puna District been enough of a challenge? Unfortunately, he had to leave behind the two hundred sheep in his flock because of his transfer. They loved their *kahu* so well that they called him by his Hawaiian name—Kamiano. *Makua* Kamiano had baptized over one hundred new converts and performed seven marriages in his first year at Puna. He had been particularly proud that three babies had been christened Damien, Catherine and Francis after him, his mother, and his father. There would now be a little bit of Tremelo, Belgium in the former district that he had traded with Father Evard. The elderly priest did not have the body of a boxer like Kamiano, the physicality necessary for his new parish.

The Kohala Parish on Hawai`i Island as drawn up by the Honolulu Diocese ran from outside Hilo all the way to Hāwī—a land area of 1,000 square miles or one mile per parishioner. Kamiano's carpentry skills at Puna were behind the bishop's decision to send him to Kohala. In his previous assignment, Damien had built two churches and five thatched hut chapels in only a few years. Bishop Maigret was impressed by the young priest's talent for constructing buildings out of a "few loaves and fishes". Perhaps the Belgian could do that in the more expansive Kohala area.

The padre with whom he had traded districts had left Kamiano a small wooden church and a "luxurious" five-room *pili* grass priest's hut in Waiʻāpuka. He used the term "luxurious" in contrast to the blanket that he slept on under a breadfruit tree his first night in Puna. The irony of his current isolation was that the parish was located in one of the most beautiful spots on Earth. A number of miles east of the rolling hills of Hāwī, St. Louis Church in Waiʻāpuka had, for a backdrop, streams that raced down some 5,000 feet from the cloud forests of Puʻuoʻumi and Kaunu o Kaleihoʻohie at the summit of the Kohala Mountains. The streams eventually merged into breathtaking waterfalls that plunged off cliffs into the turquoise ocean below. Damien thanked the Lord for his picture book parish and presumed that the local people were as *ʻolu ʻolu* or pleasant as the setting in which they lived.

He was exhausted, having traveled all the way from Kona by horseback. He promised the Lord that he'd make up his prayers tomorrow, as he detachedly tumbled into Father Evard's old sheets. The winds, muttering as they blew ashore, painlessly eased Kamiano into a deep, soothing slumber.

The morning birds sounded like giggling children, and indeed they were. Three little brown faces balanced their heads in the frame of the *pukaaniani*—humored with the notion that the new white *kahu* slept with his shoes on. Damien gave them a goofy look back, dusted his frock, and tried to dissolve the huge crease that ran down the front of his cassock.

"Aloha, kākou, ko`u kamali`i hulu," he called to the birdlike children.

He grabbed his almost empty bag of tobacco, stuffed and lit his pipe, and searched for wood to heat the stove for some coffee. The three little wise men moved from the window to the door. Only then did Damien notice that the keiki *manu* were bearing gifts.

The oldest by a hair stepped forward. *"No ke kahu, mai ka makuakāne a me makuahine."* The priest bowed at his future parishioners and, like Christmas morning in his boyhood village, the newcomer excitedly opened the sacks. Behold! Did they have some kind of predictive powers? The bags were filled with aromatic tobacco, freshly pounded coffee beans, and, after munching into one of them, the sweetest bunch of rosie apples he had ever tasted. His morning had been blessed.

"Thank God and thank your parents," he relayed to them. The children giggled gleefully as they flew off into the *hau* forest.

Luckily, it was four days to Sunday when he'd meet his congregation, hopeful that they'd be as filled with as much aloha as his Puna people. There was so much to be done. He had inherited from Father Evard some pigs, sheep, chickens, two horses, two donkeys, and a cow. Just tending to these beasts would be time consuming, so he'd need some help. He also envisioned creating a garden with coffee and tobacco plants, as well as sweet potatoes and beans.

He knew that as soon as he met his flock on Sunday, he'd be off on a get acquainted journey to all the stops in the district. He had memorized the district villages: Kawaihae, Niuli`i, Waiakamali`i, `Iole, He`eia, Pukapu, Alaula, Makalapa, Honokāne, Honoipu, Waikoloa, Nalaula, Kaiopiki, Koki`o, Makeanehu, Waimea, Hāmākua, Honoka`a, Laupahoehoe, and, of course, Kohala—the collective name given to all these villages, big and small. He would definitely be a multi *ahupua'a* priest, caring for his children, from the highest rain-swept peaks down to the rolling sea.

The Sunday sun was blazing brightly as his struggling, religious community poured out of St. Louis Church. He looked curiously *ma uka* up Wai'āpuka Gulch and noticed small plumes of smoke filtering out above the forest canopy.

"Aloha. E komo mai," poked a finger at his back. Kamiano turned to the beaming smile of a weatherworn old man.

He said in Hawaiian, "I have a canoe for you." This was followed by, "My name Kahele. Jonah, like the *koholā*."

The man's sunny disposition would not be clouded by the priest that Mr. Kahele's baptismal name, Jonah, was actually the prophet, and not the whale of the Old Testament.

"I don't think I need one," said Damien.

"You need. You cannot take Jesus some places without a canoe. 'A'ole pilikia. My sons bring 'em here till you have a place by da ocean for put 'em." He repeated his welcome, then headed to his waiting sons and *wahine*, who all smiled at the new minister.

A few days passed. Kamiano was working on the little portable altar for the donkey traveling church. He again noticed smoke up in the *'ōhi'a* and *kōlea* forest in the headlands.

"E kahu! Makua Kamiano!" Mr. Kahele's two strapping, headless sons were headed his way. They finally stopped, lifted the canoe to reveal their faces and plopped the *wa'a* on the grass.

"*Mahalo, e nā keiki kāne o Kahele.* What are your names?"

"We are the Sons of Zebedee." They proudly pointed to themselves. "Keoni—John. Kimo—James."

"Mahalo. Tell your *makuakāne* that I am grateful." He paused, then asked, "Oh, what are those fires I see above?" He pointed to the *waikele* up the mountain.

"*Ma'i Pāke...*" they said in a very reserved tone of avoidance and, with those two words, turned. "Ah, Father is waiting for us to work in the *lo'i*. Aloha." They waved until they were out of sight. Kamiano didn't understand their reserve about the upland smoke, but he would soon find out.

His first duty was to take the fleeing route of Kamehameha's keepers along the Hāmākua trail through Pololū, then Waimanu, to Waipi'o Valley. He now knew what had made Pa'ea the grand warrior that he was. Kamehameha the Great's traverse across those valleys by foot was a tough physical challenge for any warrior-in-training to face. Kamiano, however, had his trusty donkey, Hamor, whom he named after the first beast of burden mentioned in the Old Testament. The district would be traversed by Hamor in half the time it took the cleric to walk it. Kamiano would stay longer at the St. Joseph Mission in Hilo. There he would confess his sins to Father Pouzot and join in the camaraderie of one of his fellow priests for a week. Some five weeks later, he had completed the circuit and was back in Wai'āpuka.

Days passed, Damien preoccupied with the chores neglected for over a month. The heat of the day woke him one morning, accompanied by the boisterous singing of *'ākepa*. His tired eyes were once again drawn to the upland *waikele*. Smoke issued from the forest treetops. He was determined to take a long hike to satisfy his curiosity. He replaced his cassock with hiking garb, grabbed some chunks of *kūlolo* for sustenance, and started the ascent.

The climb up was gradual; he passed through some dryland and meadows, trudged through forests of *koaiʻa* and *ʻiliahi* trees until they were replaced by the thickness of the more rain-loving *ʻōhiʻa*. Looking *ma kai*, Kamiano spotted his tiny church, a mere speck in the distance.

As he moved higher, he set his eyes on a plume that billowed a quarter mile up but, as he got closer, the smoke disappeared. He no longer had a point of reference. As he ventured another distance up the slope, the forest became commandingly quiet. He took another step forward and ran into a string attached to a cowbell. The jangle frightened off a covey of quail.

"Stop. No come close!" demanded an unseen voice.

Kamiano scanned the wet cluster of *kōlea* trees. He saw a shadow behind some large ferns.

"Aloha. Who are you?" Kamiano requested.

"A man with no name."

Kamiano had some fear and trepidation that the shadow could have been a crazed person, someone in hiding from a crime, so he backed up. He suddenly remembered the *kūlolo*.

He shouted back, "I'm leaving this for you."

"What?"

"*Kūlolo!* To *kaukau*."

"Leave it there and go!"

Kamiano placed the treat on a large boulder, shouted out aloha, and started back down the mountain.

The night was quiet, but Kamiano slept restlessly. Who was this man? Why was he up there?

A mist covered Puʻuoʻumi when rooster crows echoed across the valleys. Kamiano was still asleep, exhausted from the night-long concern that wound round his brain—the man with no name.

As Malia Manawaleʻa approached the priest's hut, the *noʻenoʻe* on the Kohala Mountains seemed to quickly dissipate.

"Good morning, *kahu*. I'm finished with the church. I'll be leaving now. Everything stay ready for Good Friday Services. You sleep okay?" said the church helper.

"Good morning, Malia. No, unfortunately I didn't. But perhaps you could make me sleep better tonight if you can answer my question before you leave"

"What is it?" asked the woman in her fifties.

"I noticed fires *ma uka*, so the other day I ventured upland but was halted by a shadow in the trees. I asked several villagers, but they refused to talk about it."

"You must be careful, *Kahu*… " She stopped short, and changed the subject. "But I have so much to do." She turned to leave. He trailed after her.

He persisted. "Malia, I ask you, for the sake of God, who is that man?"

"I don't know which person. There are a number of them that live among the trees and in the caves."

"Are they the *kauā*—the outcasts?"

A tear came to Malia's eye. "Not by their deeds, but their disease."

"What disease? I have help in my bag."

"There is no cure for *maʻi Pāke*."

"A Chinese illness? Is there another name?"

"The white man calls it leprosy. But you must stay away, Father. If you touch them, you will get the disease! Oh, sorry, *kahu*. Have to leave… so much work." She turned and hurried past the ti leaves and down the trail.

Kamiano called from the distance, "Who is the man with no name?"

"My son," she called back, disappearing over the horizon.

Holy Week came, and as Damien washed the feet of Malia and the Kahele boys in the Holy Thursday service, he was determined to head up the hill with some food to give to the man with no name. The priest had not realized that the scourge of leprosy had hit the island. No one had spoken aloud about it, not even his fellow priests. Perhaps they, too, had been filled with the fear of the *ma'i Pāke*. Perhaps they believed that if they came down with the disease, then they would be of no help to their flock. And how many were in hiding? He had counted at least five fires above him up at Pu'uo'umi. Multiply that by the many other peaks and valleys of the Kohala Range as well as the flanks of Kīlauea, Mauna Kea, Mauna Loa and Hualālai, and the number of lepers would be considerable.

Since he was a boy, Easter services had meant something special to Damien. It all came together: the warmth of spring, the family get-together, good food and the confirmation of life beyond as recalled in Jesus' resurrection. And so it was thousands of miles away from Belgium with his new *hānai* family. Yet even the joy on the faces of his adopted parishioners, as they received holy communion, could not erase the priest's concern as he stared out the St. Louis Church window up at the small *ma uka* fires. He was determined to take the trek that day and make a second attempt to reach the heart of the man with no name.

Several hours later, the spring sun, the gentle tradewinds, the scent of dewed ferns caressed the cleric as he trudged up the trail toward Puʻuoʻumi. Damien, in his cassock, with his doctor's bag in hand, finally neared the spot where he had been told to go no farther.

The command in Hawaiian was the same this time. "*Hoʻopau!* Stop! No come forward!" said the shadow in the trees.

"I know of your illness and I've come to talk," answered Damien in Hawaiian.

"For your own good, it not good for you come close."

"I know about the *maʻi Pāke*. Perhaps I can help you. I've brought along a bag of medicines."

"This disease no more cure, contagious."

"That I know, but I can help you with specific problems—constipation, toothache, whatever... " said the priest, then added... "As long as I don't touch you, I'll be fine. Can we at least talk?"

"Nothing for talk about."

The *makua* was almost lost for words. "Ah... perhaps we could talk about Malia."

A long pause was followed by, "Malia? How you know Malia?"

The shadow was no longer a shadow. Leprosy had disfigured the man's face to the degree that Kamiano could not exactly tell his age.

"She takes care of my church."

"You are Father Evard? I thought you more *makule* man. You young."

"Can I come closer? I wouldn't have to talk so loud."

"Sit on the tree stump; that's where Ma... " the man with no name abruptly stopped. Damien concluded that no one should know that the man's mother was secretly visiting her son.

"I'm not Father Evard. Yes, he was older. He has gone to Puna, and I've replaced him. Aloha. I am Father Damien, Kamiano in Hawaiian."

"I'm surprised you *haole* but speak Hawaiian so good."

"I learned it fast when I was stationed at Puna. I had to or I'd starve. Luckily, God has also given me a good memory."

The man with no name was obviously nervous when he finally uttered, "How is Malia?"

"Fine. She is the sunshine of our church. When did you see her last?"

"About a week. She as busy as a widow can be. She sits where you are sitting when she comes and brings *kaukau*."

"Oh," the priest responded, "that reminds me. I almost forgot. Here." He poked his hand into the bag he had carried up. "Some fresh bread, some *kālua* pork and…"

"I no can take that, Father."

"It's Malia's creation. Father Evard turned her into quite a baker."

"Well… Poke 'em through the hole in the fence… Listen, Father. I no like be one burden on anybody. Look in back of my *hale*…" Suddenly, the leper gagged on his phlegm; white spittle formed at his mouth. He hacked until the mucous was free and spit it into a container. Damien's heart felt the burden as much as the man. "I'm sorry, *Kahu*. It's just…"

"No need to explain. What about the back of the house?"

The ill one continued. "As you can see, I try to be my own man as possible. I have a plot of upland *kalo*, some sweet potatoes. The forest have some tasty fruit, and sometimes *pua'a* wanders into the area. That night I feast on pig!" The cough that had attacked earlier resumed. The leper hoarsely apologized, "I need for rest."

Damien agreed with him and gathered up his belongings. "Oh, before I go, here's some ointment. It'll get rid of fungal infections." As he stuck his hand through the *puka* in the fence, Damien noticed how close he had come to touching the hand of his new parishioner. This was the first meeting. Talk of God would come after the needs of humans.

"Aloha," Damien called to… "Oh, by the way, what is your name?"

"Na`a…!" He stopped mid-name at the thought of shouting it out and finished softer, "Na`amano."

"God bless you, Na`amano!"

"Likewise, Kamiano." The priest smiled at the thought that at least now he had a name for the man on the mountain.

Damien had wished he could spend more time with Na`amano, but his district was huge. Rather than getting frustrated at the almost impossible task, he decided to leave it in the Lord's hands. His time was spent on building some chapels at some of the farther outposts. The people could sense if the church's commitment was soft. Wooden churches with steeples and pews and bells were definite signs that the Sacred Heart Fathers were here to stay.

The plans for the new churches kept him away for several weeks. When he returned, the constantly whipping winds of winter had ceased, and a loving, balmy spring was in full bloom. He headed quickly to Father Evard's apiary that the new priest had expanded. Under the cool Hawaiian plum trees, he carefully pulled out the sliding trays not to disturb the fanning mumbling hum of hundreds of honey bees; he planned to take some of the near-purple honey to Na`amano.

The next morning he performed his more abbreviated mass to his regular goers—the Sons of Zebedee—and some new catechumens from Pololū. After he bid them a good day of fishing, Kamiano grabbed his sack of food and his medicine bag and headed *ma uka*.

When he reached Na'amano's shanty, he was not greeted by the usual warning. The forest was as quiet as eucharistic adoration.

"Na'amano! Are you here?" called the priest. There was no answer.

"Na'amano!" he called again. Finally, a slight groan came from the interior. Damien circled the front barrier to the back. He pushed open the door of crude wood. The leper lay on the floor besides his cot, his breathing heavy. The man with *ma'i Pāke* looked up upon hearing the creak of the door. His eye expanded in disbelief, and he mumbled in shock, each word taking enormous effort, "What... are... you... doing... in here..., *kahu*?"

"Save your energy," encouraged the cleric. He took out a wooden stethoscope from what some parishioners called his *'eke ho'okalakupua* or magic bag.

"What... is... that?" the leper tried again.

"A fancy word for a thing to check your inside." Kamiano bent over to listen to the man's lungs. He didn't want to tell the suffering man that they were filled with fluid. Damien was sure that this wasn't the first time Na'amano had suffered from pneumonia, that God had saved him from several previous bouts with the affliction.

He struggled to lift the patient, but the fit priest finally got him upon the cot. He plopped up the drool-stained bag that served as the leper's pillow so that he could breathe better. Kamiano grabbed the wooden bucket and headed out to look for water. About a hundred yards up the slope, he came upon a vivacious little stream. He hauled Adam's Ale down the hill, grabbed some kindling from around the dwelling, started a fire, and filled the almost black teapot to the top with the fresh *wai*. Finally, he extracted from his bag some fenugreek seeds, added some fresh purple honey, and brought the homemade tea to a good boil.

"Jesus tea, I call it." He blew on the hot brew. "Here, drink."

Na`amano struggled speaking again. "Who… this… Jesus? Is he… *akua*?"

"The most powerful *Akua*, Na`amano. He was a man-God who loved and cured lepers. He waits for you in the next life when you will be clean again… Do you want to accept him?"

A haunting smile formed on the leper's face. "If this be true… yes."

"Sip more," encouraged the priest. "You must drink this tea at least four times a day until *pau*. The bucket is full of water. I'll leave a stack of kindling and the Jesus tea seeds here and come back to see you as soon as possible."

"I… I… " the leper tried to say something.

"No need to talk now. Rest." The priest grabbed Na`amano's shredded blanket and stretched it over the man's body with the intent that Damien would replace the soiled cover with his own newly sewn one on his next visit. He pulled the garden vegetables and smoked meats from his food bag and left them along with his praised honey on the small bedside box.

Finally, Damien pulled out a small bottle of holy water, soaked his thumb and made a sign of the cross on the forehead, eyes, ears, nose, lips and heart of the man who once had no name. "I bless and baptize you, Joseph, *in nominee, Patris et filie et Spiritu Sancti. Amen.*"

As Kamiano made his way down the hill, he was determined to return the next day to take care of the serious ailment that plagued his patient. However, tragedy struck the area the next morning when a canoe overturned in violent seas and several parishioners perished, never to be found. The priest spent the day consoling the grieving family survivors.

About five the following morning, Damien was awakened by the ominous gossip of night birds. He was up. He staggered onto the porch and lit his pipe. The smell of burning wood wafted down onto the church grounds. The odor made him look upward. There was a large fire up the mountain! "Oh, no." he thought. He hoped... He grabbed his coat to combat the chilly morning air and headed up the slope. As he neared Na`amano's dwelling, what he had feared was true. The makeshift shack was on fire.

Staring at the licking flames was Malia, and, to her sides, stood the Sons of Zebedee, shovels in hand. Their shocked, hypnotic gaze at the blaze did not change at the sudden appearance of the priest. Damien was not upset at the thought that Na`amano should have had a normal Christian burial. He understood that the leper and all the material he had come in contact with would be decontaminated by the purifying flames, and his upland parishioner cremated within. Kamiano knew that when he had last visited Na`amano that there was little time left. He only wished that he could have had more time with the man who now had his name.

Damien hugged Malia and put his hands on the shoulders of the budding young men.

"*Mahalo*, Father," said Malia in a barely audible voice, "I arrived in time early this morning. He could barely move his lips but whispered, 'Father Kamiano said that Jesus will make me clean again.' He then stopped breathing. Was *pau*. I hurried back down the mountain and got the boys for come help."

The dwelling was now a smoldering heap of charcoal. The boys worked the shovels around until the ground was fairly level, burying not only the smoldering embers with dirt, but also the life of one leper.

A handful of mourning doves chased each other outside the window of St. Anthony Church in Wailuku. Eight years had passed. Damien stared up at the West Maui Mountains and the billowy clouds that collided with its peaks. The bishop had gathered all his clerics together with the hope that two priests would volunteer for a special assignment. Bishop Maigret got to the point quickly and bluntly.

"The territory has gathered, with more to come, all the lepers from the islands and isolated them at Kalaupapa on Moloka`i. We need to tend to the spiritual and human needs of God's inflicted children. I know that this is a difficult request... "

During this brief appeal, Damien recalled Na`amano, now Joseph, and the other men with no names who struggled, isolated, in the uplands. In his heart was hope, hope that a day would come when there would be no more fires on Pu`uo`umi.

Damien raised his hand.

THE BIG L
Ka Lā Nui

"Tony, you get one quarter?" Rico fumbled through the gum wrappers, matchbook covers, and lint in his pockets. "Otherwise, I cannot go movies with you."

"You wen check Mrs. Yamashita's piggy bank?"

"Yeah, only get Canadian pennies."

"So I guess you cannot go see *Manhattan Melodrama* with me tonight."

"What? you would go without me, your best friend, your right hand man, for see Clark Gable?"

"Yeah. Sad. Times tuff."

"Leave your *compadre* home on a Saturday night in happening Lahaina town?"

"Uh, hu. You neva heard about President Hoover's Depression?"

"Kay den, act like dat." Rico continued to pick through the disaster where they slept in search for one thin quarter, one-fourth of a dollar.

Tony and Rico were not their real names. They had gone to the movies so often that they had taken the names of gangsters they emulated. Tony had taken his alias after seeing Paul Muni in *Scarface*. Rico, of course, had taken on Edward G's name from *Little Caesar*.

They were really Elwood and Egland Dang, otherwise known as the Dang Brothers. But even that was fallacious. Oh, they were both Dangs, but they were not related—as far as any paperwork was concerned. However, like masters who have the look of their canine companions, the constant camaraderie of the Dangs created the impression that they had emerged from the same mother.

The movies they saw from morning to night were indeed escapism—their modus operandi for avoiding any serious employment. Oh, they had worked... until they were fired—usually for sleeping on the job or pilfering unlocked supply cabinets. To cover their irresponsibility, they sometimes bragged about the number of jobs they had "retired" from. Interested observers estimated that it was in the double digits, but who was counting? Their quitting or firing was always much to the joy and relief of both employee and employer.

Both their fathers had worked on ships out of Canton and had bid *bon voyage* to Maui as fast as they had impregnated and bolted from expecting mothers. Both boys had been entrusted to the good nuns at The Maui Children's Home in Pā`ia before the infants knew better. They became cohorts in laziness when they both were enrolled at, and eventually kicked out of, Lahainaluna and the dorm for stealing pockets full of prophylactics from the Pioneer Mill Clinic, blowing them up to decorate the principal's office, then setting his swivel chair on fire. After questioning the boys, the local truant officer reported to the head of the school what the juvenile delinquents had to say about the deed. He said they showed no remorse when they described the crime scene adorned with rubbers as "party-like and gay", and the smoldering vinyl chair smelling "jell like incense". After being kicked out for the balloons incident, the hooligans disappeared into the

Lahaina jungle to survive on their own; they emerged several months later as boarders at Mrs. Yamasaki's, a stone's throw from Māla Wharf.

"Rico?"

Rico halted his search for silver. "Yeah?"

"Have you ever wondered like me why you so *lōlō*?" asked Tony.

"I tink my mother dropped me when I was small. Ass what she told Sister Mary Assunta at the orphanage," Rico answered, but retorted. "Why? You figured out how come you so mental?"

"I read in the *Maui News*... " said Elwood, changing the topic.

"Egland, you cannot read so no try act all high *maka maka*."

"Hey, I told you before—no call me Egland... it's Rico. You can make fun, but at least I wen finish *Fun with Dick and Jane*... so I not as itinerant like you."

"Anyway, before you wen interrupt me," continued Tony, "I said I was reading the words I knew in the *Maui News* and saw that one Doctor named Fraud from the city... what's the one that makes the little sausage?"

"You mean Libby's?"

"No. Vienna, Vienna. See, you wen interrupt again. Anyway, this psycholologis said you can come *lōlō* from your parents... you know, it's hermidity, so not yoa fault."

"Yippee," interrupted Rico. He pulled a quarter from a knotted handkerchief from Mrs. Yamashita's *Toscani* box and sang and danced around the bed, finally prancing onto the sagging mattress in an ecstasy of silver—the coin held high like a tiny Olympic medal. He began to sing:

> *"We're in the money, We're in the money,*
> *We've got a lot of what it takes to get along.*
> *We're in the money, the sky is sunny,*
> *Old Man Depression, you are through,*
> *you done us wrong."*

"Okay, so now we can go movies tonight. I hope you happy, but what we going do till 7:00?" said Tony.

"What we usually do, drink."

"You spent one-half hour looking for twenty five cents, now how much *bia* you think we can buy with that?"

"Look, you gotta be more invective and try figure out some adda ways for get beer," insisted Rico.

"You mean like go visit Old Man Morreira?"

"Less go."

Old Man Morreira was the only guy with money in the area. Everyone had left town to work with the WPA on the Hāna road. Morreira took a physical retirement from the train for gout and spent most of his pension on brewing homemade beer that brought in steady money even during Prohibition. As of the first of the year, Prohibition had been officially repealed so Old Man Morreira was now on the verge of selling his famous brew, which he often tested, usually for hours on end.

The duo jumped on their bikes and headed up toward Wahikuli. The old man's plantation house rested comfortably under some large mango trees, a Rudy Valee record blaring from the Victrola just inside the porch window. Old Man Morreira sat on the verandah, coddling one of his brown bottles. Upon spotting the advancing duo, he slurred under his breath, "Oh, oh, here comes drouble."

"What, Morreira, you taught of one name for your *bia*

yet?"

"I dunno. Why? You get one good one?" the old man said, almost knocking his beer bottle off the railing.

Tony looked at Rico with a message in his eyes. "Duck soup. This guy stay feelin no pain."

Rico's suggestion was, "I know one foa you." He imitated a radio ad. "When you taste *Ōnō Bia*, you say *Ōnō*."

"Ass stupid. Should be grand… like *Maka Pia Bia*—You see 'em—you drink 'em."

"And who made you one advertisement guy, Mr. Smarty Pants?"

Old Man Morreira stopped the debate, "What you guys doing hea? Came leach as usual?"

"Ho. You know fo hurt one guy," said Tony.

"We just came for samples, now that you going get rich, what now *pau* Prohibition," apple polished Rico.

"Oh, I gotta admit dat moa fun drink with udda guys den by yorshelf," said the Old Man as he rose and crossed to the screen door. "I like you taste my new batch." After fumbling with the door handle, he finally entered and continued shouting, unseen to the Dangs, "I've got one hundred cases ready to go. My daughter in Kaimukī should have one label next week." Old Man Morreira burst back out the door. Elwood and Egland looked at two cases of beer held by the brewer as if stunned by a beatific vision.

"And don't think I'm giving dis to you because you nice. I just wanna get drid of you runks." The Old Man dropped the two cases of beer onto the porch. "One for each." He left for a short time again, as the boys slapped and pinched each other to see if it was true. The beer meister replaced Rudy Valee's crooning with Harry Epps Crackerjax banjo-pickin' music and then burst through the screen door like the Second

Coming, decreeing—"But this is for us now." Old Man Morreira had, gripped in his withered hands, another case of the home brew. He stared at the two wannabe gangsters and, with the innocence of an altar boy, posed the sacred question, "Anybody get one church key?" The two boys, without thought, simultaneously drew their Blatz bottle openers like swift swords.

Time passed, each ten minutes marked by another empty bottle on the verandah railing. The drinking marathon came to a halt at the sound of the eleven o'clock whistle blasting from the Pioneer Mill. The signal stirred them from their hops-and-barley stupor and resurrected new life in Tony and Rico.

"How about one for the road, Johnny?" suggested Rico to the now passed out drunk.

"I think stay the end of the day for Old Man Morreira," replied Tony.

The host was posed in a contortion like a Hindu god, snoring through his open mouth.

Rico jumped up with the energy of a second wind. "Whoo whee! Let's hit the road like Bonnie and Clyde, with two cases fo go."

"Hey, Pretty Dumb Floyd, Bonnie and Clyde neva rob banks on bikes," insisted Tony.

"You think Old Man Morreira going mind if we borrow his car?"

Tony asked the coma-like Morreira in mock politeness, "Excuse me, you no mind if we borrow your car?" The Old Man snorted a distorted, "Whatevers."

"We'll bring 'em back before we go to the movies tonight. Promise," added Rico. The tipsy drinkers slowly slipped the keys to the Model A out of the brown slacks of the drowsy Morreira, giddily hid their bikes in the cane field across the driveway, ran to the dilapidated garage, jumped in the two-door beauty, and peeled their way down to Lahaina town, the banjo music from the Victrola fading in the distance.

The warm February trades filled the Model A as thoughts of Al Capone and Baby Face Nelson swirled through their heads. Rico pulled up two beers from under his legs, gushed them open, and handed one to Tony.

"'Ōkole maluna!" Rico saluted.

"Double cheers," said Tony, clinking the bottles.

"Damn good beer if I no say so myself," said Rico.

Tony daydreamed out the window for a short while until his eyebrows formed a serious look.

"Rico, you like me?—You tired of being pua?"

"You know," said Rico, "I was jess thinking da same ting."

Tony continued, "I know we not going eva win one Academy Award or the Purple Cross or one spelling bee. We going die pua."

"Or we can do what Cagney and Bogart did," suggested Rico.

Tony made a sharp left onto Waine'e Street and parked the car between a bunch of mango trees to go undetected.

"Where we going?" asked Rico.

"We going eat lunch," said Tony, with no need to explain.

Mrs. Yamashita, who worked part-time at the Liberty Restaurant on Front Street, saw the infamous twosome through the windows that looked out to the Lahaina Sea.

"What you guys doing hea?" They tried to kiss her, but smelling the alcohol on their breaths, she pushed them away. "I taught I told you guys for leave Mr. Morreira alone." Despite her no-nonsense ways and understanding of their negligent upbringing, there was a small part down in the hair trap in the dungeon of her heart that cared about these misfits.

She carried on with her diatribe. "If you would spend moa time lookin' foa one job den drinking, you could pay for this lunch and your three months late rent. Gunfunit! You guys like sponges." She brought two glasses of water to their table and yelled out to the cook, "Chun Hoon -Two fried soup!" She then scraped her slippers to another table with newly arrived customers, looking back to give the dropouts a final pre-meal stink eye.

Rico scanned the spartan restaurant and stared, like he always did, at the picture on the wall of flowers that had little girl faces.

"I'm in it, if you are!" stated Tony.

Rico asked, "In what?"

"We rob one bank, Rico!"

Rico slammed his hand against Tony's mouth, staring over at the table with the other customers. "Shhhh!. You *pupule*? Why don't you blab 'em to the *Maui News*."

Chun Hoon, the cook, emerged with the fried soup and plopped it on the boys table, wiped his sweaty brow with his apron, and returned to the kitchen.

Tony took Rico's advice and continued in *sotto voce*. "Like I told you in the car. I tired of being pua."

"We going get caught," insisted Rico. "Get one guard in the Wailuku bank, and they going know us in Lahaina."

"Dat's why we do one small bank whea dey nevah know us."

"Like whea?" asked Rico.

Mrs. Yamashita looked over at the boys. She had never seen them so intent in conversation—much in contrast to their usual silliness.

"What about Pā`ia? Stay right off the street. We go in—we go out. I heard only get two tellers and one the manager."

Rico agreed by nodding his head as he slurped up his fried soup. Tony insisted that Rico leave the quarter that he had pilfered from Mrs. Yamashita's cigar box as a tip for the generous lunch. "No need quarters. In a couple of hours, we'll be, as you always sing, *In the Money*." The boys headed out the door, posing a mimed thank you to Mrs. Yamashita as they left. Squinting at the glare of the Lahaina noon, she curiously quizzed them, "Where you guys going?"

"Checking out a job!" Rico yelled back. Mrs. Yamashita looked at the quarter tip with suspicious familiarity and knew from the top of her head comb down to the bottom of her flip flops that the duo was up to no good.

"Gunfunit," she blurbed.

The two retrieved the car from its hiding place and raced back onto Waine`e.

"Where we headed?" asked Rico.

"We gotta get some bank robbing duds," explained Tony. He suddenly had an idea as he passed Smokey Botelho's Embalming Studio. The place was closed, Smokey probably off to another part of the island to pick up a body. When he was there, with a Lucky Strike dangling from his lips, Smokey would always spill out one of his morbid puns like "my business stay dying" or "everybody dying fo see me," before he slapped you on the back like a choking victim. "I'll be right back," said Tony as he stopped the auto, ran off, and returned with a couple of black mortician suits.

"If we're going to be Maui's first bank robbers, we gotta travel first class and look like Cagney and Bogart," insisted Tony.

The boys turned into Mrs. Yamashita's driveway unaware that Mrs. Gomez, their next-door neighbor, was adding bluing to her whites and staring from back of the latticed porch at the troublemakers' new found wheels. In fact, it looked like Old Man Morreira's Model A. She also saw them stash one of the cases of beer under the porch behind the *ti* leaf hedge.

Inside, the wannabe robbers downed a couple more beers, donned their costumes and struggled with ties which they had never experienced, the accessories eventually evolving into distorted black nooses.

"They going know us. We need one face disguise," suggested Tony.

"What about bandanas?" was Rico's proposal.

"What? You like look like Al Capone, one gangsta, or Tom Mix, one cowboy?" said Tony, rummaging through a Dutch Cleanser cardboard box.

The rejected suggestion was replaced when Tony rediscovered a pair of scratched up dark glasses from an old purse that the two had finger lifted from some tourists tanning near Jodo Mission.

Wiping sweat from his brow, Tony added, "And this." He snapped up Mrs. Yamashita's eye brow pencil and grabbed Rico's face.

"What the he…" protested Rico.

"Stay still," commanded Tony. "You need one mustache. I'll give you the Adolph Menjou look." He then moved over to the mirror and created his own curlycued handlebar. Both stared into the mirror, visually denying that they looked more like over-heated Mormans than cool gangsters. They mopped up their foreheads as Tony led the charge, "Pā'ia, here we come!"

"Wait a minute, Tony, what about a rod… and a note… a bag?"

Tony faked, "Oh, yeah. I was jes going bring dat up! Hey, I think Mrs. Yamashita's nephew when leave his water gun here. I taught I saw 'em under the mango tree by the swing. You go get 'em while I write the note." Rico left, confused at the thought that his buddy could read, and returned with the water pistol stashed inside his coat jacket and a nearly empty rice bag for the loot.

They stuffed their normal clothes into an Ichiki Store sack to change back into after the heist, raced out to the coupe, grabbed a couple of warm beers from the case back of them, and headed out on the road to Pā'ia.

The day seemed to warm another degree as they passed Puamana, the flats at Olowalu, the Pali, and, within an hour, Haleakalā Highway to Pā'ia. The east side of the island was no cooler. The black bank robbery costumes would have been the right choice for breezy Chicago, but not for the eighty plus degrees of a Maui winter's day.

The angels with *no mo* wings passed the bank several times to scope out the situation. Pā'ia was immobile, having been drugged drowsy by the flood of molasses in the air. They decided to go up to the sugar mill, turn around, and pull curbside to the bank. One step off the sidewalk and they'd be in the door, then quickly heading back to Lahaina.

Having just arrived from the Philippines, Florentina Balabag had been on the job for only four days. It was her aptitude with numbers and her blood relationship to the manager that got her the job, and not her mastery of the English language. Her cousin, the manager and alternate teller, Margarita Foo Sum, had gone to the outhouse in back several times that morning; she was in her eighth month. Luckily, she was in seclusion when the robbers stepped into the bank.

Tony stepped up to the cage.

"Good - morning, - sir," Florentina said in the regimented

manner learned from Cousin Margarita. "Can - I - help - you?"

Eyeing the terrain, Tony pushed a note across the counter toward Florentina. She picked it up and quizzically looked at it. The illiterate note read, "This is a hole up. Give us all your muny!"

She put her palms up to either side. "I do not know this one?! Maybe I get Margarita... "

"No Marguerite," he snarled at her like George Raft. "Give money!" Florentina was further perplexed, having never experienced American gangster movies much less a hold up.

"Show her your gun, Rico," growled Tony, his bravado melting when Rico pulled the red water pistol out from his pocket along with the rice bag, the remaining contents of the latter splattering to the floor like a wedding exit.

As she said "red gun" audibly in Filipino, Florentina's eyes bulged, finally having realized that they were *banditos*. She peered for Margarita out the back window, but the little sign on the bathroom door still read "occupied". She had no choice but to give the cash to the two perspiring Mormons with fake mustaches. Rico stuffed the dollar bills in the rice bag, and they scurried out to the car. The Dangs expected a shootout like Cagney would face as they burst out the door, but the only action they encountered was a perspiring stray mutt limping down the sidewalk. Tony grabbed for the keys in his pocket, then uttered, "Oh, my God!" He realized that he had left them on the counter. He dashed back in only to re-shock an already woozy Florentina Balabag about to make a yelp for help toward Margarita. He snatched the keys, uttered a mangled "thanks eh", and retraced his footsteps out. The car was off and running as Margarita made it back from the toilet. The Ford raced down Baldwin Avenue toward the ocean.

"Bank robberies sure make you sweat. I gotta get out of these clothes," insisted Rico.

"Relax," said Tony, his heart still pumping like a wound-up drummer. "We'll stop by Uncle Roy's place in Sprecklesville. He get one outdoor shower, and he work da day shift Pu'unene Mill." They drove down to the end of the driveway unaware that Uncle Roy, one of Elwood's many short lived foster parents, was home from the sugar company fighting a kidney stone. He heard the car, peered out the drawn curtain, and saw the rapscallions peel off their mortuary suits. As naked as mynah birds, they hopped around the shower, trying to douse their dastardly deed down the drain. As they changed back into their undershirts and slacks, they guzzled a few more beers, saluting each other at the successful job. The black suits would eventually be tossed, along with the silly red toy gun, off the Pali cliffs. Uncle Roy watched them swerve back onto Hāna Highway toward the West Maui Mountains; he would only have to wait to see what was going down with the infamous Dangs.

The boys were passing Olowalu when a police officer arrived at the scene of the crime. A somewhat bewildered Florentina Balabag gave the officer information between snivels and shivers, Margarita seeming ready to give birth with all the excitement she never witnessed. An all points bulletin was issued.

Mrs. Yamashita, at the same time, had caught a ride home as usual with the day cook, Chun Hoon Kam. He would return later to usher her to *Manhattan Melodrama*. She went *loco* when she stepped into the unlocked house.

"Gunfunit!" she screamed. "This place look like one typhoon when hit 'em." She turned on the radio to Bing Crosby singing *Let Me Call You Sweetheart*, the song in contrast to the venom that flowed as she checked for missing belongings.

"That's eet! Dey *pau*," she bellowed when she opened her Toscani box. "Dey stole my quarter for go see *Manhattan Melodrama*." Her shriek brought her neighbor, Mrs. Gomez, huffing and puffing.

"What they did?" was followed by a "You okay?"

"Gunfunit. They up to no good," belted Mrs. Yamashita.

Mrs. Gomez volunteered to stir the pot. "They left in one car."

"Dey no have license. Cannot be."

"Can be. The car look jus like the kine Old Man Morreira have," suggested the neighbor.

"Dat's it. They went get him drunk and steal his car; I hope for onee joy riding."

When My Ship Comes In on the radio was interrupted by a KMVI announcer. "The Pā`ia Branch of the Bank of Hawai`i on Baldwin Avenue was robbed at gunpoint by two assailants at high noon. An undisclosed amount of cash was taken, according to bank teller, Florentina Balabag, 'by two men, maybe six height wearing dee funeral suits with a sweating, not real mustachio… oh, and red gun.' No one was harmed during the daytime heist according to investigators. And now here's a rebroadcast of Hollywood and Broadway news with the *Walter Winchell Report*." Mrs. Yamashita turned the nob to off and raced to the telephone to inform the police, afraid that the boys might get hurt in their craziness.

The winds at the Pali minus the black monkey suits seemed to cool and calm the now notorious duo. They gleefully tossed two quickly downed bottles and popped open a second set.

"So where we gonna hide da money?"

"I thought maybe Māla Wharf, but get too much people."

"Up da mountain no moa people," suggested Rico.

"Perfek!" thought Tony. "We'll bury the stash under the L."

"Da L?"

"Yeah, you know—the L up the mountain from the school we was kicked out from."

"You some smaat. Nobody stay up dea. And you know what, Tony?"

"What?"

"Going be easy for find da money because L stand for Loot."

Luckily, Old Man Morreira's Ford was used only to go to the church and the market. The auto borrowers conquered the mountain without difficulty, grabbed the sack of dough from the trunk, and took the final trail to the Big L—the large letter proudly tended by the Lahainaluna senior boarders that could be seen from all the lowland areas.

Rico and Tony were giddy with the amount of money they'd pull out of the bag. They extracted two beers that Rico had thrown into the same sack, doused the monetary contents on the ground, and began their attempt at simple counting. Tony scribbled the sum in the red dirt after some doubtful re-checks, officially proclaiming a total of $976.41.

"Is that good?" questioned Rico.

"For one hobo like you dat never saw $1,000, dat's damn good," said Tony as he stuffed a bunch of twenties in his pocket for splurging that night.

After Tony buried the rice bag under the L, the two sat, sipping their beers, staring out at distant Molokaʻi and Lānaʻi sitting in an ocean of glass. It was a peace and freedom they'd never experience again.

Tony finally broke the staring silence, "Well, my pahtna in crime, we now gotta celebrate our successful job. We gotta get some broads."

"From whea?"

"What about the Gonsalves girls from Puʻukoliʻi? Dey always like good fun."

"Dey kinna big," said Rico.

"An you kinna ugly—so match," ribbed Tony. "We takeʻem dinner at that new classy restaurant—The Banyan Inn—and den go movies after."

"What about the car? We gotta take ʻem back."

"Old Man Morreira stay in lala land. We takeʻem back right after we drop off the girls."

"And what about our clothes?" Rico insisted. "We can't go to the Banyan Inn and act highfalutin in undershirts and sweaty pants."

"You're right," added Tony. "What we need is a couple of nice tropical print shirts and white pants like high *maka maka* tourists wear."

"Tanks for giving me one good idea. The musicians at the show at the Pioneer Inn!" announced Rico, happy with having come up with at least one suggestion.

Tony steered Morreira's car down the alley back of the Pioneer Inn and alongside the open window of the entertainers' changing room. Rico hopped out of the car, ran over to the pier, swiped a pole from a snoozing fisherman, and caught, off the clothes rack, two shirts with palm trees and hibiscus, two pairs of white pants, and, with more difficulty, a couple of pairs of white shoes. They raced off to the ballpark, dressed in the dugout, wet down their hair, finger brushed their teeth at the drinking fountain, then headed up to Puʻukoliʻi to get the Gonsalves girls.

The girls were as their mother politely described them— big boned. The Amazons, as Rico otherwise described them, were always up for a good time, despite the quarantine their mother imposed on them. She felt they were too loose and would end up pregnant before they were eighteen, like her. Colette was tying up the dog when she saw the car approach the house. She raced for Yvette.

"It's the Dangs in a fancy car!" yelled Colette.

Mother Gonsalves heard the hormonal frenzy and yelled out at them, "You not going out with those hoodlums, so forget it!"

Mr. Gonsalves emerged from the garage smoking a cigarette to see what the fuss was about and was immediately harped upon by his wife about his detestable tobacco habit. She howled at him deliriously; he called the usual diatribe—"the wailing of the banshee". The sermon about the deadly outcome of "inhaling Phillip Morris" was followed by a homily on the permissiveness of Mr. Gonsalves, who eventually took the stand in the debate that his daughters would not get knocked up. The battle that waged between the parents gave cover to the girls who, during that lengthy verbal volley, were able to change, grab their rouge, lipstick, and hairbrush, and escape.

"We'll be home after the movie," they yelled gleefully out the window, as they headed down the hill to Lahaina town.

"You girls are up for a treat tonight," spoke Tony, smoothly. He flashed a couple of twenties. "We're going to the Banyan Inn for dinner, then we'll meet Clark Gable at the Queen Theater." The girls squealed with joy, each grabbing the brother closest to her, noting from the matching shirts that the boys had finally gotten a job with a Hawaiian band.

Meanwhile, the Sheriff himself, Clem Crowell, had responded to Mrs. Yamashita's phone call. He interrupted her and Chun Hoon who were listening to *Fibber McGee and Molly*, but not laughing tonight.

"Oh, Clem, so good to see you. Have you found the boys yet?

I'm afraid that bank robbery in Pā'ia is their *huhū*. Somebody dey stealing from maybe get itchy finga and shoot dem. Your boys not going hurt 'em, eh?"

"We won't, Tamiko. Maybe prison will shape 'em up, learn 'em a trade. Now, the teller at the bank saw them leave in a Ford Model A, which we haven't spotted yet. I can only get two men out here tonight. You have any idea where the boys might be?"

"I'm sure they going movies. Get *Manhattan Melodrama* tonight. Chun Hoon and I going."

"You shua they going be there?" insisted the Sheriff.

"Dose guys leeve and breed movies. And now dey going movie prison for being dumb dodos."

"Well, listen. We'll stake the theater. You talk to them sometime during the movie so that our boys will be able to i.d. them and pick 'em up outside the Queen. We don't want no fuss; this ain't Chicago."

"Tell yoa boys I going be wearing my red *mu'umu'u*. Cannot miss."

The girls were in for a treat; the Banyan Inn was mostly for rich tourists, a luxury for most locals. The foursome were greeted at the door by a replication of a female lei greeter from a Matson travel poster; a waterfall of plumeria cascaded down the side of her grinning face.

"Alooha!" She bedecked the bank robbers and their molls with strands of crown flower. As she giddily welcomed them, Rico commented almost inaudibly, "Ho! I feel like da pope."

"You look like da pope," responded Tony who then directed his demands to the hostess, "We'll take a table with an ocean view. I'm sure the ladies would love it." Collette halted her scratching to mumble, "Oh, yeah."

Tony looked across the room to the waiter at attention

near the table with the ocean view. He cringed. It was Malino Malapit, another street hustler aware of the duo's spotty past. The toothy hostess seated the foursome, the other three oblivious to Tony's concern about their waiter.

"So, Egland, how's it going these days?" asked Malapit.

"It's Tony!" Egland insisted, lifting his collar like Paul Muni.

"Yeah, whatevas."

"You know this guy, Tony?" asked Rico.

"Where'd you find the dough, Tony? The same place where you usually find it?"

"What dough you talking about?" Tony turned the question to check if Malino had caught wind of the heist.

"You gotta have dough to eat at a joint like this," needled Malapit.

"His rich uncle went *make* and left him the money," fibbed Yvette as she ogled at the steak and onions being served at a nearby table. "Now can we eat? I'm hungry," she pleaded. The *niele* waiter ceased the interrogation, took the order, and returned with the tasty bounty.

An hour later, Tony and Rico and the Gonsalves girls patted their ʻōpū as they made their way out of The Banyan Inn. The meal, a feast of steak, baked potato, and chocolate mousse, had come to $35. The only hassle came from the stink eye directed from the waiter familiar with Elwood and Egland's rap sheet, still suspicious of the duo's sudden magnanimous purchases. Tony, sucking on a toothpick and wishing to avoid similar musings by familiar patrons at the theater, suggested his gang take in the now sinking Lahaina sun, walk to the Queen, then slide inconspicuously in the back row during the previews.

The decision caused consternation in Mrs. Yamashita at the theater, worried that the boys had changed their plans. This forced her to pretend to go to the bathroom during the coming attraction for *Tarzan and His Mate*. She stalled, washing and drying her hands four times, then reentered the theater.

Out of the dark of the back row Tony whispered loudly, "Mrs. Yamashita, what you doing here? Got one hot date?"

"What, with Chun Hoon? When we going to yoa wedding?" teased Rico.

"No make like dat, you guys. Gunfunit," she retorted, sinking in her seat, filled with the guilt of Judas Escariot, from the M.G.M. Lion roar to the closing credits.

And, as Clem Crowell had insisted, it was no big deal; the arresting officers in plain clothes waited for the signal—Mrs. Yamashita's red *muʻumuʻu*. She preceded the culprits as the audience poured out of the theater onto Front Street.

"Elwood and Egland Dang?!" asked the taller detective. "You're under arrest for the robbery of the Pāʻia bank." The suspects were confused for a second, their fictitious moving picture names so engrained in their vocabulary. The two girls were shocked, suddenly enlightened, then oddly titillated by the daring misdeed that led to the bad boys' temporary fortune.

"Do you have anything to say?" insisted the shorter detective.

The dialogue for the eventual day of reckoning was obvious. Tony did his best Paul Muni, "I don't know nothin'. I don't see nothin'. I don't hear nothin'. Understand?" Rico continued with his Eddie G., "Mother of Mercy, is this the end of Rico?"

Mrs. Yamashita shrugged at the boys from just outside the circle of the arresting officers. Mixed with sense of justification and guilt, she could only meekly say, "I'll send all your stuff to you." The girls blew big kisses at "their men", as they were led away.

The head cop pleaded to Mrs. Yamashita to drive the Gonsalves girls back home and then return the car to Old Man Morreira. She agreed, and Chun Hoon followed her up the hill.

Minutes later, Chun Hoon and Mrs. Yamashita dropped the Dang molls off and quickly left to avoid being caught in the middle of a world war. As soon as Old Man Morreira's car disappeared over the hill, the whole Gonsalves clan went into full battle mode. The verbal crossfire included "See, see, see!" belted out by the matriarch, words that rhyme with witch by the patriarch, and "You're all nuts" by the sinful siblings.

Mrs. Yamashita and Chun Hoon drove up to Wahikuli and found Old Man Morreira as the boys had left him—twisted like a snoring pretzel. She slid the keys back into his pocket and tiptoed from the porch, the drunken brewmeister unaware that his church car had made Maui history.

As they rolled down the hill from Wahikuli, a less anxious Mrs. Yamashita was silent, then justifying her actions to Chun Hoon repeatedly that old Lahaina would be now safe from the boys, and the boys safe from themselves. She suddenly ceased her serious thoughts about the day, blurting out an audible afterthought to a startled Chun Hoon, "Ho. I jes peety doze prison gahds. Gunfunit."

EPILOGUE

The Dang Brothers were sentenced to ten years in prison. A few months later, they escaped for several hours, were caught while eating saimin in Kalihi, and sentenced to another ten years.

The word got out a couple of years later that while preparing for the final night ceremony before graduation, a senior boarder at Lahainaluna, while digging an outline trench around the Big L that would be later set on fire, pulled up a rice bag containing $934.41. He declared it a good omen—a gift from David Malo. The money was used to create a bigger L on the mountain.

Twenty years later in the 50's, the same Pā'ia bank was robbed again, this time by a policeman faced with mounting gambling IOUs. The residents of the island eventually learned who the culprit was but kept it under wraps, more concerned that his beloved wife and children were debt free.

THE TRAIL TO MĀNĀ

Ke Ala I Mānā

When the jacaranda trees bloom and their blossoms fall like purple snow flurries along the Kula Highway, our senses and memories are stirred by their fern-like leaves and aromatic wood. The purple rain is a sign that, soon, cowboys on horses will be busting out of their chutes, and the smells of rodeo summer will fill the air.

There's quiet around the grave of the legendary cowboy, Ikua Purdy. Here in ʻUlupalakua, someone has placed an orchid lei, a symbol of his Big Island birth, on the site where he has rested since the Fourth of July, 1945. The normally quiet Purdy, however, did not always lead a sedate life. He was caught up in the world of the *paniolo* including the World Rodeo Championship in 1908, and it all started the day Eben Low lost his hand.

PART ONE

Eben Low sat on the porch of the manager's cottage staring out beyond Puʻuhue Ranch. He plopped himself down on the big *koa* rocking chair on the verandah, as he often did after a long day of work, to watch the sun slide over the mountain and down into the Kona sea. The twenty-six-year old looked beyond the South Kohala ranch he was in charge of and again admired the oasis in the distance. It was the cinder cone, Puʻuwaʻawaʻa, its flanks greened by ceiba and ʻōhiʻa trees set against the backdrop of Mount Hualālai, the Kona volcano framed by an intense azure sea and cotton clouds. He was determined to make it, that Eden in the distance, his future home.

The calm *pau hana*, the quiet after a day's hard work, caused him to nod forward, spilling his wide brimmed hat to the floor. He instinctively stooped to pick it up with his left hand. Unfortunately, he had been fooled again. He did not have a left hand. Here's how it happened.

The rains of April carried into May and, despite the dismal weather, it was time again for the Puʻuhue Ranch manager, Low, and his hardened cowboys to head out and round up the cows and bulls that had wandered off into the Kohala mountains on the flank of Mauna Kea. The lingering rains had created a number of bogs off the slippery trails along the slopes—traps dangerous to both cows and *paniolo*. Eben would head the roundup with thirty head of pin steers, twenty-five roping horses, and nine men.

As final preparations were being made to leave the ranch, one of the nine, Eben's brother, Jack, made his way out to the departing men. He stared strangely at his fellow cowboys.

"I... I can't go... " he stuttered.

"What's the matter, brother?" asked Eben. "You look like you've stared death in the face."

Jack was spooked by the accuracy of the statement. "I had a dream last night," he said. "Nah, more like a nightmare."

"Like all us humans," replied Eben.

"But... in the dream... I die," continued his brother.

Eben was a twentieth-century realist, but his Hawaiian blood rejected the notion that dreams were merely inconsequential fantasies. His Hawaiian heritage always had a place for omens and signs, and he respected that tradition, and Jack's wish.

"Oh, I'll come," added Jack, "but when I feel the time is right."

"You follow up later with half the pin steers. How's that?" suggested the older Low.

"*Mahalo*, brother. Have a safe ride," said Jack.

Eben signaled for the cowboys to head out. Along with the newer cattlemen, Eben had the best riders and ropers that Parker Ranch had ever seen. There were Ikua Purdy, Archie Ka`aua, Sam Kahalekui, John Lanakila, Robert Steven, and, when he would join them later, his brother, Jack Low, all of them, part of the Parker family clan.

Seven dollars a head was quite a bit of money in 1842, and these men and their boss were determined to gather those cattle in spite of the uncomfortable, several-days trip to Laumai`a. They stayed one night at Pōhakuloa, traveled along the southwest forest of *māmane*, hunkered down near the Humu`ula Sheep Station for a day's rest, then continued their journey along the side of Mauna Kea, facing Hāmākua and Hilo with its legendary rains.

Laumai`a was an unusually flat, treeless grand meadow at the 10,000 foot elevation—a magnet—a perfect grazing location that lured cattle and bulls. It was also a convenient, unhindered roping area surrounded, unfortunately, by a dense tropical rainforest of *koa*, `*ae*`*ae*, high `*ama*`*u*, *pālapala* trees, among others, and thick hedges of *pulu* fern. Once the cattle ran or roamed off the meadow, they were often trapped in the devouring bogs—harmful to the herder, even more harmful to the cow, who usually died after considerable stress trying to free itself from nature's snare. Most often, the cowboys, familiar with the final outcome, left it or killed it, taking back the valuable rawhides.

After a rest on the eight thousand foot level, the cowboys, looking like foul weather monks in rain gear, plodded up the slippery trail to Laumai`a. Eben noted the *kēhau* or cold that penetrated the air. Their plan, done many times before, was to leave the pin oxen at a lower level to avoid scaring off the vagrant bovine and to bring the roped runaways down to them. The loose cattle would then be tied to the domesticated pin oxen, the latter creating a calming effect on their wild brothers for their trip back to Pu`uhue Ranch.

"As usual," Eben whispered to the boys, "try no make noise."

The nine cowboys and their horses knew the instructions, silently made a procession up the trail, and slipped into the *kōlea*, `*ōpiko* and *rapala kēpau* trees awaiting the appearance of strays.

In the meditative quiet, like his men, Eben thanked his horse from his heart for being so smart and loyal and dependable. He ran his hand over his animal's mane and rubbed his neck gently, reminding him that he didn't want him to be hurt. As they rested and waited, Eben could feel the horse's heartbeat, its muscles tightening in anticipation of the coming action.

The rain stopped suddenly and, with it, the chatter of insects in the high grass; some four-legged creature was nearby. It wasn't a cow, however. Out of the morning mist appeared three ornery-looking bulls. Eben brought the no-make-noise finger to his lips, then counted with his fingers. On three, the men charged out from the forest shadows onto the flat. Eben tore after the brute who veered to the left. He almost had the big horned beast down when his horse stepped onto some soggy logs, plunging *lio* and rider into the mud. Ikua Purdy and Archie Ka`aua reigned in their bulls, and the remaining men went after and captured Eben's escapee.

Everyone took a break from the rigorous seizure, then continued to round up cows and move them into the adjacent five-acre stonewall paddock that had been laid out years ago. The untamed were then attached to their tamed counterparts. By the time the sun set, Eben was happy at the well-stocked pen. With brother Jack's probable arrival the next morning, the group would gather up the few remaining wild cattle, tie them to the pin oxen, and, hopefully, head back to Waimea by late afternoon.

A *noe noe* drizzle drummed on the canvas tents all night and rhythmically hypnotized the tired men into a deep sleep.

The sun wakes up early on the top of mountains, and so do cowboys. Despite the soggy situation, the men rose, splashed their faces, then jovially devoured biscuits, sausage, and Mrs. Low's "nobody's sleepy anymore" coffee. The waxing sound of spurs and moans of the pin cattle signaled that Jack was here.

"We gotta get that one big cow that moved to higher ground at the flat at Waiki`i yesterday. He's the Menotaur of the meadow," noted Eben, recalling the Greek legend from his childhood history book. "Sam, you go get em."

"I'll do it," volunteered Ikua. "I saw the fire in that cow's eyes."

"Nah. I can handle, Ikua," insisted Sam, and he started up the trail.

"Ikua, go help Jack bring up the pin oxen," ordered Eben.

However, after he sent Ikua off, Eben had second thoughts about that exceptional beast with the rebellious attitude. He sent the reinforcements, Archie and Robert, after Sam and Ikua to help them move the aggressive cow down the slippery, narrow cut in the rain forest. Soon, they were back with the bruiser. One of the pin steers was brought close to be coupled to the stray, but as soon as Sam removed the rope from the captured's neck, the cow charged him. The veteran cowboy tried to gather the lariat up as fast as possible, but he was too late. The cow, luckily, however, stepped with its forelegs into the coil of rope. Seizing the opportunity, Sam pulled hard, and the animal's chin bit the dust. The dazed beast had a mean streak of determination and, as soon as he got back on his feet, he lowered his head, compelled by the devil to do some damage. Archie came to the rescue, this time lassoing the demon's rear legs. It caused the wild one to crash to the ground, again. His stunning fall brought some temporary peace to the *diablo*.

Eben mumbled his concern about "bussin up the poor cow", then instructed that all loose ones be attached to Jack's recent arrival of pin oxen. Finally, they'd start their two day trek back to Puʻuhue Ranch.

"Move 'em out," called Eben. The caravan of cowboys started their descent in single file down the sloppy trail. Eben personally escorted the behemoth at the rear on the right of the path. Suddenly, like a stirred up funnel cloud, the possessed cow bolted again. This time he careened down the slope, dragging his pin oxen mate in tow. Eben spun a hoop around the lunatic and, if the beast had gone straight down the trail, Eben's powerful anchor, his steed, would have stopped the errant cow dead in his tracks. However, the crazed animal crossed over to Eben's right and coiled his tether around three *māmane* trees. The usually alert Eben Low would have normally shifted the rope from one hand to another, but, sadly, the rope caught his fist at the pommel, and the rawhide rope sliced him at the wrist.

Blood gushed from the dangling fist. Ikua looked back at the evolving chaos and raced to Eben's side, shouting, "I'll get a doctor. If you move out," he told the onlookers, "take the Keanakolu trail to Mānā. I'll meet you with the doctor part way." Ikua raced off. He would have to ride thirty-five miles as fast as he could to the doctor at Honoka`a.

Archie would become temporary doctor. He cut off a piece of leather and created a tourniquet. It worked; the bleeding stopped, but the normally rugged cowboys shivered when they glanced at the mangled, drooped wrist. The arm was then wrapped in bandages and delicately placed in a sling made from a large bandana. Eben was in shock but managed like a seasoned general to give the orders, "Move `em out!" Everyone obeyed, realizing that they had to meet Ikua and the doctor sooner than later.

Luckily, it was Ikua that went. He knew that backcountry better than anyone else, all the shortcuts as well as the obstacles. All night he rode and reached Honoka`a at 4:00 a.m. He pounded at the doctor's door, irregardless of the time.

"Dr. Greenfield! Dr. Greenfield!" he shouted.

After a short while, a drowsy Mrs. Greenfield appeared, lantern in hand. "Ikua, what's the matter?" she queried at the emergency.

"Where's Doc, Mrs. Greenfield?"

"He's in Hilo," she stated.

"Oh, no," said Ikua. "Cannot be. Hilo?" Ikua thought that gangrene would set in if he had to ride even farther to Hilo.

"Is anyone hurt? Who is it?" insisted the doctor's wife.

"It's Eben. His wrist has been sliced," said Ikua, now in a dilemma.

"Oh, my God, the poor man." Mrs. Greenfield offered some

consolation. "There's a Japanese doctor down the way, about seven miles, at Kukuihaele."

Ikua raced over to his horse, leaped on him, and shouted back at Mrs. Greenfield to telephone Dr. Veddick in Kohala and have the surgeon meet the returning party at Mānā, a rough halfway point. He would take the Japanese doctor with him to temporarily attend the stricken Low but was certain that surgery was inevitable.

Mrs. Greenfield ran to the phone, one of the few on the island, and called Kohala for the surgeon.

Mrs. Veddick, the surgeon's wife, answered the phone, herself having just put her drunken husband to bed.

"Eben… his hand severed?" Mrs. Veddick was upset that Eben was in dire straights. "Meet at Mānā? Okay." Mrs. Veddick raced to the cottage in back and pounded on their part time assistant/blacksmith's door. "Johnny, Eben's cut his wrist severely. We've gotta get the Doc up. Do all you can to get him to Mānā as soon as possible."

"But we just put him to bed…" said Johnny.

"To hell with him. If that lush can drink, he can ride… and besides, he's Eben's best friend. He'll thank us when he's sober," insisted the surgeon's wife.

With the help of the two, Dr. Veddick was pulled from his spinning bed, force-fed cups of black coffee, and tossed onto the buckboard, the doctor unaware of his destination.

A sweating, exhausted Ikua and the Japanese doctor met the cowboys with the paining Low at Hopuwai at 4:00 a.m. Despite a language barrier, the physician performed his basics but admitted that surgery was the ultimate decision, with the caveat that he was not trained to perform such a delicate task. Ikua, in the meantime, advised the group that arrangements had been made to meet at Mānā, where Dr. Veddick would be waiting, so they'd best head out before Eben's situation grew more critical.

The purples of pre-sunrise were splashed in various shades across Mauna Kea as the band of cowboys and the ailing Eben Low came into Hanaipoʻe. The sparse inhabitants, awakened by snorting horses and the moo of cattle, dressed quickly and attended to their familiar friend. The girls, including Helen Parker, gathered up new bandages to replace the utterly soaked ones.

"Could you get me a *poi* cocktail?" Eben drowsily requested in the middle of the chaos. The attendees looked at each other quizzically.

"*Poi* and milk," Archie interpreted.

The group laughed. "Of course, Eben," Helen said as she ran off to the kitchen. The *kalo* cocktail seemed to do the trick.

The long, bumpy buckboard ride to Mānā fortunately knocked the aftereffects of booze out of Dr. Veddick, who finally realized where he was headed, and why. Within the hour of the surgeon's arrival, the round up crew and the patient filed into Mānā. The care for his best friend became Dr. Veddick's stimulus for sobriety.

After a thorough examination, noting the onslaught of gangrene, the specialist decided to cut, not above the elbow where another surgeon would have, but below it. It was risky, but Dr. Veddick knew that if the bend in the arm were saved, Eben still could have a limited, though continuous, career on the range. After opiates had been given time to do their job, Dr. Veddick finally removed Eben's hand, and with thanks to the Lord, he claimed success!

Fifteen years later, Eben was standing in the White House about to shake hands with another rough rider—Teddy Roosevelt. Eben had received an invitation from the president. The chief executive had written to Low; he wanted to meet Hawaii's famous cowboy if Rawhide Ben was ever in Washington. It was during this period of his life that Eben had the itch to travel, and it was on one of these sojourns that he decided to "stop by" 1600 Pennsylvania Avenue.

Eben presumed that, once he met the president, he'd go through that awkward dance of explaining why he couldn't shake his hand, that he—well, he'd have to tell the whole story, again. He was impressed, however, when Roosevelt used his other hand to greet the renowned Parker Ranch *paniolo*. The president had obviously done his homework. Like veteran cowboys, instead of a campfire, the two settled down to swap old stories of buckskins and broncos in front of the fireplace at the White House.

On one of his stops while returning to Hawai`i, Eben Low attended the World Championship Rodeo in Cheyenne. Eben sat there, impressed by the American cowboys, but more intent to believe that his boys like Ikua, Archie, and his brother Jack were superior to the Mainland *caballeros* and would do well if they were to enter. He made his impression vocal when he got into a teasing discussion with a bunch of local Wyoming cowboys after the bronco-riding event.

"Not so fast," said Angus McPhee, one of Cheyenne's great cowboys who shared something in common with Low. He only had one arm. "Kind of risky sending your boys here and embarrassing all the folks back home! I've got a better idea. We'll come to Hawai`i and challenge you on your own turf. If you win, or at least prove that your cowboys have the muster, I'll heartily endorse your entry into Frontier Days competition next year."

Eben accepted the challenge. Angus McPhee did indeed come, and his boys did beat the *paniolo*, but barely. Angus, nevertheless, kept the second part of the deal. He felt that they would be able to at least compete, even though they didn't dress, act, or ride like the American cowboys. Low sold his ranch to finance the trip. He would take three of the best—three that showed their love the day Eben Low lost his hand.

PART TWO

San Francisco was still under construction when Eben arrived by steamship at The City with his best riders: Ikua Purdy, Archie Ka`aua and his brother, Jack. The great earthquake had occurred two years prior to the Hawaiian cowboys' anticipated showdown in Cheyenne, but The City, still in rubble, could not deter the Hawaiian visitors who were awestruck by this special place—its magnificent bay, rolling hills, brisk air, and alternating sun and fog. Their weeklong journey from Hawai`i had exhausted the travelers, so they looked forward to a restful night before catching the train to Cheyenne, the next day. They loaded their belongings onto a wagon and headed up to the Opal Hotel on Van Ness.

Needless to say, the boys hit the sack for a nap until awakened by nearby evening church bells. They shaved, slicked down their hair, tucked their bright, long sleeve shirts into their washed blue jeans, and headed to John's Grill down on Ellis for, as Eben put it, "a mighty `ono steak dinner." After their feast, they spilled out into the streets, patting their satisfied `ōpū while sucking on toothpicks. The air was cool but tolerable as they reached and strolled down Van Ness to get a better view of Alcatraz, looming in the bay.

The day shaded from blue to black and, within the hour, the temperature dropped into the 50's, so the men trudged back up the hill to their hotel. Everyone was in a jolly mood but concerned about Jack's wheezing—a sign of an onslaught of his occasional bout with asthma. It would bother him during the rest of the journey and into the competition.

The fog was still hugging the Barbary Coast the next morning as the foursome made their way on the ferry to Oakland. Then, they'd catch the Union Pacific and make their way through Reno, Salt Lake City, Ogden, and, finally, Cheyenne.

The locomotive, nothing akin to the sugar cane trains back home, chugged its way north under the California sun, and, in a few hours, it was hugging the foothills of the Sierra Nevada. The men were awestruck by the service on the train: the *pleases* and *thank you, sirs*. They were equally shocked by the prices on the dining car menu after they stuck their noses into the rolling restaurant on the first night of travel. They drooled over the salads, prime rib, coffee, cakes, and pies served on starched, virgin napkins. Despite considering the $10.00 cost of dinner as lunacy, the cowboys were determined to have a fling and live life on top for once. They returned to their car to finish their prepared tuna sandwiches, dreaming of the following night's banquet.

The train came and left Ogden by noon—the men leisurely spending the day watching the western states go by. Six o'clock rolled around, and as the sky turned indigo, the train made its way across the Great Salt Lake. The hungry travelers sniffed their way to the big *pā'ina*. The dining car porter blinked several times when he thought he saw a couple of brothers make their way to a table. He was amazed how they so casually examined the menu, oblivious to the curled lips of some of the other patrons.

"What state you boys from… Alabama, Mississippi?" asked the dining host.

"We're from the territory," stated Eben.

"I didn't know there were Negro folk in Arizona?" quizzed the black man. The men laughed, the host reacting similarly but without reason.

"Oh, we're Hawaiians," stated the three, almost in harmony.

"Well, Hawaiians or not," said the porter, "if the white boss comes through…"

"No need to explain," interjected Eben, having experienced the lack of aloha in some sectors of the country on previous trips. Some nearby diners continued to peep prejudice over their menus, but the men took Eben's advice and ignored the gawking, claiming, "It's their problem, not ours." Luckily, the white boss never came.

The moon came out and the train seemed to glide across the Great Salt Lake like a skating snake, parting the waters like a biblical miracle. Its vastness gave the men the time to consume a hearty meal before the locomotive pulled into the Mormon capitol in the pitch of night. The train stopped briefly, just a day away from reaching their destination and their destiny—Cheyenne.

The clock tower at the Cheyenne depot clanged 9:00 a.m., the city ablaze in sunlight and packed with cowboys arriving from ranches east and west, a-hootin' and a-holerin'. The town of thirteen thousand would swell three times before the end of the week. The cold of San Francisco had changed gradually as they crossed the Rockies, the temperature now hitting the century mark in Wyoming's Capitol, much to Jack's relief.

They jumped off the train in their slouchy hats, bold shirts, and even brighter bandanas. Suddenly from the crowd, a voice called out, "Alohaaa. The rough riders are here!" A woman, lei in hand, raced up to the arrivals, bedecking them with red carnation garlands and, at the same time, christening Ikua as Mauna Kea, Archie as Mauna Loa, and Jack as Hualālai. The Hawaiian cowboys were taken aback—convinced that they were lost in anonymity on this bigger island.

"Now, you're probably saying: who is this crazy Hawaiian woman?" giggled the greeter. "Ikua, I am a Napu'upahe'e, your wife's cousin from Kawaihae—Hattie."

Ikua gave the cheerful *wahine* a big hug. "You give me chicken skin, Hattie. We never expected any kind of greeting. It's so good to get the reverse aloha spirit we give all the time."

Hattie brought forth a bag. "Now be careful. Was hard to find flowers around here, but I did the best I could." She pulled from the sack four *lei pāpale* for their hats. "If you keep it in a cool place, it should last for the week." The four men started to feel a lot more comfortable. Hattie went on to tell them that she and her husband had moved to the continent when he had a chance to work for the Union Pacific Railroad. She suddenly halted in her conversation, as the men gathered up their belongings, and teasingly asked, "Where your horses? Didn't they ride with you on the train?"

Eben quickly interjected, taking the joke more seriously. "We just couldn't afford to ship them, so we're going to have to borrow." The men were most concerned about this. It could be a huge disadvantage working with unknown horses. Eben quickly de-emphasized the negative by insisting, "I don't think Angus McPhee will give us a couple of *lio* ready for the glue factory."

"Well, I know you guys gotta go get settled, so I better *hele*... oh, so nice to say Hawaiian words, and especially around handsome Hawaiian guys. I see you after you win," Hattie declared, disappearing in the steam blasts of an engine leaving the station.

Angus McPhee was waiting at the hotel. "The *kanakas* have arrived!" he bellowed. "Aloha, Hawaiian cowboys! Welcome to Waiomina! Did I say it right? I've been practicing." The boys gave him thumbs up. "Not gonna stay long—I'm sure you boys are tired and hungry. Just wanted to welcome you to Cheyenne and remind you that we'll meet at the Frontier Park Stables tomorrow morning at 6:00 a.m. to choose your horses and gear and do the necessary prep and practice."

"As long as no ʻoʻopa," warned Eben.

"I didn't catch that one in the Sandwich Isles. You'll have to fill me in."

"Lame, Angus, no lame horses."

"No way, Eben," Angus chuckled. "I promise. Now, go get some good grub and some shuteye. Tomorrow's a big day. Hell, this week's a big day. Aloha, *paniolos*," said Angus as he broke out into the blaring sun. He returned and warned, "Oh, and ignore anything you read in the papers."

The rough riders considered it merely a cliché until they reached their rooms, dropped their bags, and fell backwards on soft beds. Archie was the first to show up at Eben's door with complementary copies of the state newspapers. "Look, boss!" He slapped the back of his hand against *The Denver Post*.

Eben couldn't believe his eyes. The banner headline read: "Beat the Browns!" At the same time, as if on cue, Jack and

Ikua knocked and entered Eben's room, noting that Archie had beat them out of the chute.

"At least they got the color right," needled Ikua.

"No use getting *pupule* over a piece of *pepa*," encouraged Eben, the motivator. "By the end of the week, they're going to have to change their headlines." The men humbly agreed and joined their hands in a Hawaiian victory clasp.

Hundreds of parade viewers, along with Eben Low, gathered along Capital Avenue for the opening Parade of 1,000 Cowboys. Eben was thrilled by stagecoaches, the D.A. Russell 1st Cavalry, the lady cowboys, and filled with pride when his three friends clopped past him on their borrowed horses and saddles. The parade eventually spilled into the Cheyenne Frontier Days grounds, and so began the eighteen events scheduled for each day. The Big Island cowboys had to work on their patience and composure; steer roping would be the thirteenth event.

Jack's bout with asthma caused by the San Francisco cold was replaced by a new catalyst—Cheyenne's six thousand foot plus altitude. The young Low, though, never complained, keeping it to himself. Although he never moaned and vowed to make Hawai`i proud, his fellow cowboys knew him well enough to know that he was not up to his usual spriteliness. Eventually, by the end of the week, Hualālai, with a faint wheeze, would nevertheless end up sixth above hundreds of cowboys. Even Archie, his hand paining from a previous accident, managed to make a good time, lassoing that calf in one minute and twenty-eight seconds. In that heat, Ikua managed to bring in his steer in at one minute and seven seconds. If he beat that in his final try, he would indeed be a world champion.

The *paniolo* could not sleep that night. They tossed and turned, realizing that with Ikua they could change history, that the mainland cowboys would no longer make fun of their hats, clothes, and style. It would be a salute to all the working men and women ranch hands of Hawai`i.

Jack, the man of omens, noted that it was a sign of good luck that an unknown cowboy named Dick Stanley had moseyed into town, signed up for the bronco riding event, tamed the infamous, unconquerable black stallion, Steamboat, and hightailed out at sunset, leaving his trophy behind. "Us foreigners going do good!" predicted Jack.

Eben sat with Hattie and her husband among the 10,000 spectators in the stands, Archie and Jack along the fence near Ikua. Purdy had one last chance to pass the roper in the number two position. A huge hush came over the crowd as they and Ikua waited for the release of the steer. The cowboy was easy to spot and follow, his large floppy hat glowing from the Big Island red of Aunty Hattie's *lei pāpale*.

A gunshot cracked the air. Ikua, like a Fourth of July rocket, shot out in a near-perfect straight line, toward his fame. The steer didn't even have time to issue a moo before it was tackled and tied, all under a minute. The crowd jumped to its feet and roared like a mighty mountain lion. Tears of joy, satisfaction, and pride rolled down Eben Low's face, his body sandwiched, squeezed like a wrestler from the tag team of Hattie and her burley husband. After a pause of after-shock, Eben raced gleefully toward Ikua and the boys along with Angus McPhee for some joyous jumping. Eben excused himself from the revelry and darted to the telegraph office.

The agent at the *kelakelapa* office in Honolulu received the good news: "To: *Pacific Commercial Advertiser*, *The Hilo Tribune*, *The Maui News*, *The Garden Isle*—stop—Hawaiian Cowboys win World Rodeo Championship in Cheyenne—stop—Ikua Purdy breaks 1904 record—stop—fifty six seconds—stop—Archie Ka'aua places second—stop—Jack Low places sixth." Eben walked out into the Rocky Mountain sunlight, proud that he had played a part in the honor that these cowboys brought to Hawai'i, convinced that it would live past their last roundup.

After the big hurrah, the Hawaiian champions returned to parades and parties across the islands, a style of life that they put up with for a while, but their humbler callings made them most eager to return to the content of normal, rugged work on the range.

Jack and Archie returned to their lives as cowboys on the Big Island, until they moved on to that big rodeo in the sky.

Upon his death, the cowboy descendants of Eben Low took his ashes, as he had requested, to the top of Mauna Kea, his beloved mountain, and scattered them to the wind, never to again face the hard rains of Kipu'upu'u.

After his return to Hawai'i and a stint on Kaua'i, Ikua was lured to 'Ulupalakua Ranch on Maui, where he proudly worked in relative anonymity until, as his humble monument shows, he died on Independence Day, 1945.

And while today's cowboys parade down Makawao Avenue every Fourth of July, not many miles up the winding road rests Ikua Purdy. With Kīhei under his feet and the mighty Haleakalā for a pillow, Hawaii's greatest rope man once again, in spirit, lifts his now smooth hands to touch the soft rain of jacaranda blossoms; and his now creaseless face inhales the sweet scent of eucalyptus. Visitors to the spot are reminded once again of a cowboy bound to his brothers, not by rope, but by memories of aloha.

THE TEENAGE CREATURE FROM THE BLACK LAGOON

Ka Mea Ola ʻŌpio no Ka Kaikohola ʻEleʻele

The King Theater in Wailuku was in chaos. It was another spooky doublebill and the musty old venue on Vineyard Street was bustin' full of kids. Mr. Furtado walked down the aisle, trying to force out the creases from his brown, let's look professional, sweat-soaked, official-announcement suit coat, while being subjected to a multitude of incoming near misses of popcorn and Jujubes boxes.

He slowly turned, and with enough volume to awaken the dead in the St. Anthony Church graveyard, yelled at the top of his lungs, "Shuuut uup!" The children went cold turkey from a din to monastic silence. The weekly ritual then proceeded with the movie ogre making his way up the aisle, the silence giving way to murmurs, the murmurs to talk, the talk to yelling, and the yelling to renewed chaos and flying wet crackseed bags.

The Menace chuckled to himself about the way kids acted without their parents; he himself would not engage in such behavior, aware that a *koa* stick would leave a red imprint on his `ōkole if his parents had caught wind of it.

Screams poured out the door onto Vineyard Street as the lights dimmed. It was a '60s re-release of two 3-D classics: *The Creature from the Black Lagoon* and *It Came from Outer Space*. Besides scaring The Menace and his friends with their B movie sets and bad acting, Universal had also provided the *li hing mui* and butter fingered patrons a cheap, easily destroyed pair of 3-D glasses that, when used, resulted in red-green headaches. The Menace looked to the back of the Takitani theater and noticed, through the barrage of *manju* and licorice wrappers, the girl with the `ehu hair munching on *mochie*, and staring in his direction. She stood out in contrast to her fellow, geeky, freshman girlfriends. The couple exchanged a few awkward stares.

It was in a post movie, only-boys-allowed meeting at Dairy Queen while munching Dillies and checking the sticks for free ones, that the Creature from the Maui Lagoon was hatched. The German, who was actually Portuguese and who would eventually play the beast, came up with the idea of a beast rising from the depths of some Maui bay to terrorize an innocent beach party. It would take time to develop a credible costume and set up the right conditions like some prank from *Candid Camera*. If nothing else, the boys would have the girls stalked by an wanna-be Oscar winning fiend who would cause them to desperately run into the secure arms of boys to men.

October was here. On a sleepy little island in the 1960s with three hotels and TVs producing more snow than an occasional winter's day on Haleakalā, one would think that a teen's life was boring. But The Menace and his gang had a busy weekend that included a homecoming game on Friday evening and a dollar-a-car night at the drive-in on Saturday.

The following weekend was the Maui County Fair, where the whole gang would meet on Friday, the appearance of the Creature from the Kīhei Lagoon scheduled for the haunting hours of Saturday.

The Menace had been puzzled by his inability to get girls. In the movies and television that bombarded his teenage libido day and night, everyone seemed to have girlfriends. Was it his looks? Couldn't be. Even pocked face gangsters had molls. Was it his body? He did have a third world country poster boy look about him, but, hey, even Arnold Stang was married. The Menace's only conclusion was confidence or the lack of it. He pledged that in this senior year, and in particular this weekend, he would change his attitude and take on the aura of James Dean. More importantly, he had to confirm the true intentions of the girl with the ʻehu hair.

On Thursday night, The Menace waited to be picked up by The Bird, the former's nickname associated with the precocious Dennis of the comic strip, the latter from his chatter like a myna bird. The Menace's father claimed that costly insurance was the reason his son would have to wait until he was eighteen to get his driver's license. With that card, akin to James Bond's killing permit, The Menace could finally get a steady. Of course, some of the other boys had faced the same dilemma. To solve the problem, those who had no money for wheels ended up towing home abandoned heaps that had once littered the edge of the Waikapū Dump. Those cars were held together by Elmer's Glue, rope, and a prayer. One could actually see the road whiz by through the floor of the car that the Bird had hauled home from Apana's Junkyard. Dennis regretted his dependency on catching a ride with friends, his guilt minimized, though, because teens feel comfortable traveling in packs, like wolves.

Besides The Menace, The Bird, and The German, the other members of the boy's gang, Hi Ho (a salute to the Lone Ranger's Portuguese horse), Mario (his grandfather's name), Dishes (his dutiful excuse for not going out with the boys) and Gorge met at the Andrews girls' house to shred paper to create the necessary blizzard for an intensely prayed-for touchdown at the following night's predictably doomed game. They used the Andrews' house as the staging area because, well, the Andrews girls were five of the best lookers in America's newest state. The beauties taunted the overflow of male teenage hormones. The boys felt, talking among themselves, that it was at least better to be near beauty even if they couldn't have it. But, back to business. This would be no ordinary blizzard but a senior year extravaganza with enough confetti to fill a refrigerator cardboard box from Hamai Appliance. When the mission was finally accomplished with brute fingers and grade school scissors, the gang settled down to munch on *ampan* donuts, chug down Orange Exchange Base, and flirt with the Andrews girls. It was close to midnight when Lovie Andrews, the sweet but stern matriarch, approached and swung open the front door, peered through the openings of the sprawling monkey pod tree branches in Pu`unene, and announced her overused, though easily interpreted hint: "Aye. I just saw the bread plane fly over!" The urgent announcement was a declaration that it was late! The Aloha Airlines flight, christened by locals with that name for hauling in thousands of freshly baked loaves for early morning Maui breakfast tables, had made its last flight of the day from Honolulu.

The next night, Black Gorge's carburetor was acting up. He resigned himself to the fact that he'd be a little late getting to the Kahului Fairgrounds with the huge box of shredded confetti. Gorge, who wasn't black but brown, had been rechristened by the gang with the name of a ravine, off of the side of bigger ʻĪao Valley, called Black Gorge. The gang claimed that the ebony profile on a slope was indeed that of their friend. He would eventually lose the title, however, to mythic claims by tour drivers who thought they saw John F. Kennedy's profile appear in the same spot following a landslide on the day the young president was shot.

The Bird was waiting at the entrance of the fairgrounds, the game about to start. The school bands blared from within the stadium in anticipation of the alma maters and the opening whistle. The Kahului Fairgrounds was already an old relic, built after the turn of the 20th Century. On the Kīhei side of the field was the covered grandstand that stank of cigars and leaky urinals, the rest of the track and field surrounded by ten tiered wooden bleachers.

"Hurry up, Gorge! The game's going to start!" yelled Mario as Gorge parked on the Christ the King Church lawn.

"Sorry, sorry, I'm late. Here, everybody, get a corner of the box," demanded Gorge.

The Menace stood by in a daze, wondering if the girl with the ʻehu hair would show up. Hopefully, she wasn't home with her parents listening to the game on KMVI.

The boys tried their best to carry the shaky Amana monolith across Puʻunene Avenue amidst a beehive of arriving patrons, cars, gawkers, and a hand-waving policeman. As if scripted sabotage, at mid-street, the boys lost their grip, and the box toppled over creating a winter-like blizzard in the middle of balmy Kahului. The rookie cop did not recall anything in his job description or academy training about taming a paper maelstrom. Cars on both sides of the street stopped and stared at the flurry of *Life* and *Look* magazine snow. Through the confetti flurries, The

Menace spotted her—the girl with the ʻehu hair—looking like a winter fantasy in a Christmas globe.

"Get it up and atta hea, you guys," interrupted the policeman, casting The Menace out of his lovesick trance.

"Okay, okay," squawked the Bird. "We trying."

Despite objections by the ticket taker, who was Dishes' uncle, the huge box was finally allowed into the stadium just as the *Star Spangled Banner* filled the air.

As predicted, there were no Trojan touchdowns up to the half time gun. To combat depression during that scoreless period, the contents of the Amana box were hurled into the air for any reason including one gained yard or a time out. The masochistic fans, by the end of the evening, seemed to be suffering from a case of serious dandruff, except for three *makule* alumni, veterans of the litter wars, who came prepared in kerchiefs, topped by umbrellas.

The Menace had been scoping the female situation. For some reason, he wasn't attracted to the girls in his class. They were almost like sisters; he'd been with them since they were all taught by the nuns. But the freshman peaked his interest. Happily, he spotted the girl with the ʻehu hair again. He didn't know if she was interested but he, nevertheless, summoned up his gumption to make an attempt.

The half-time show was a caravan of Chevy and Ford convertibles, borrowed from the dealerships, that carried the waving, Vaseline-toothed division queens and their escorts around the track.

The only highlight during the second half of the game took place off field when drunken Old Man Perreira tried unsuccessfully to mock the uncomfortable cheerleaders and got cocked cold by the toweled fist of Little Maxie DeRego in front of the whole crowd. Everyone agreed that the jerk had it coming. The game continued lopsided, the boredom forcing the boys to meet behind the bleachers. The girls peered down suspiciously at the convocation of the Maui teen rat pack. The German declared the project on schedule and guaranteed satisfaction with his re-creation of the monster. They returned with poker faces to their confettied seats to watch the game end sadly in a double digit to zero runaway score. Murmuring the mantra, "Oh well, maybe next year," the alumni, students, and fans dragged their *slippahs* across the stadium's red dirt out the exit, munching the remaining boiled peanuts, their heads held high. Like dedicated Cubbie fans, the Trojans had learned long ago how to live with pessimism and defeat. The Menace, however, didn't end the night like the Trojan diehards. He looked across to the exiting throng and spotted the object of his affection. She winked at him.

A week passed, and a bambutcha harvest moon now reigned down over the Maui County Fair. The gang associated the cane-smoked, red tinted, celestial body with the fifty plus year event as they rolled their cars into the caked parking lot, a spill over area of nearby, stinky Kanahā Pond. They sauntered through the huge multi-bulbed, stone and concrete gate which could have been any county fair gate in the U.S., its brightly lit main entrance off of Pu'unene Avenue a grandeur to a local kid like The Menace, who had never eyed the lights of Las Vegas.

The fair meant more to The Menace than a mere amusement park. It made him part of something bigger. The fair was the oldest in the state, first starting at the turn of the century up at tiny Wells Park in Wailuku, at the end of the train line. The second installment was at Kahului, its current third life at the War Memorial Complex in Wailuku. The old Kahului Fairgrounds was a romantic place, in the broadest sense of the word, for all ages. "I never see you since the county fair," had been part of Maui's dialogue for years. For the adults, it was a time to revisit the aunties, uncles, and friends from Upcountry or Hāna who ventured out of their confines once a year with a prize-winning pig, quilt, or guava jam. For teens, it was a time to hang with the gang, to be seen, look cool, and meet boys and girls. The Menace had hopes for tonight. He'd been slipped a small note earlier that day in the school cafeteria while he and his friends devoured a double lunch of Vienna Sausage and gravy. The note read, "Meet you at the fair." A face topped by curley locks drawn by a red pen, with the word "love" underscored, indicated that it was the freshman girl.

The boys made their way along the grounds, which consisted of two avenues intersected by several cross streets. The main promenade was a potpourri of typical mainland fair food booths: hot dogs, hamburgers, corn on the cob, and cotton candy, among others. The Hawaiian palate was equally satisfied by the food concessions with its own native twists: *chow fun*, teriyaki on a stick, beef stew and *poi* and *lū'au* plate.

The German, Dishes, Mario, Gorge, The Bird, Hi Ho, and The Menace went looking for the senior girls, at the same time taking in the sites with running commentary. "Can you believe he's going with her?" "A little heavy on the makeup and tissue in the bra." The first stop was the Homemaking Building that did double duty as a dance hall on weekends and, later, as the home of Maui Community Theater. It was pure Debbie Domestic in that building, and the only two reasons a male might be caught in the confines was to praise his wife's blue ribbon plum jam or to sample Mable Ogawa's oatmeal cookies.

Past the cannons that defended the fairgrounds from an

invasion from, oh, perhaps, competitors from Oʻahu's 50th State Fair, was the Art Salon. If homemaking scared the boys, there was nothing more intimidating than the word *salon*, a venue with paintings and photographs. The gallery was quiet enough to hold meditation, and the boys learned early on to stare at the painting, cup their trigger finger and thumb at their chin, nod to one side and utter, "Interesting." Outside, the real opinions ran raw from "What the hell was dat?" to "My dog coulda done bettah."

Up the side street was the Agronomy Building. Over the years, the latticed structure was dominated by stunning displays of orchids and *bonsai*, soothed by trickling mini waterfalls. The boys, almost in procession, crossed the street toward the Hawaiiana Building, which normally served as a boxing ring but, come fair time, was transformed into old Hawaiʻi. The normally boisterous boys turned monastic as they entered the past, the quiet caused by an acoustically absorbing carpet of *hāpuʻu* or fern shrub. A full size *hale*, an old-fashioned grass shack, was reconstructed every year, surrounded by a loose stonewall, framed by tall *pandanus* trees. Tables ran along the walls, decorated with an array of carved *poi* bowls, trays, and cups of *koa* and mahogany created by the inmates up at Olinda Prison. The last two buildings before the midway were the Agriculture and Small Livestock. The former had giant breadfruit from Kaupō, bigger cabbages from Kula, and the sweetest bananas from Waiheʻe. The small livestock building was inhabited by bunnies and roosters, blue, red and white awards hanging on the cages like ribbons on beauty pageant queens.

The senior girls were hanging outside the telephone booth in front of the police shack.

"Where you guys been?" asked Centa. The boys cowered at

the Amazon woman's demands.

Hi Ho took on the challenge. "Why, bahdda you?" All the girls laughed.

"We've been waiting for you to take us on the rides," said Kodish. She had been given the name from insisting that the boys not use the Portuguese reference to the devil. The attempted ban was nil; the boys used the word even more frequently to agonize Kodish. The girls, as they had planned, grabbed on to one of the boys, Sharon Ballbarrens warning Mario that it was not love but pure entertainment that she and the other girls were seeking.

Sharon Ballbarrens harassed The Menace. "Where's your hot date for the night, Menace?"

The Bird quickly came to the Menace's emotional rescue. "His girlfriend not heah yet—you know dose young ones."

"Robbin' the cradle, eh?" chimed Doler and Brownie.

Just as the girls finished their dig, the Menace's dream lover appeared from behind pink clouds. The Menace braced himself, snatched her away from the cotton candy booth, and before any more snide comments were made, the couple disappeared into the midway.

The E.K. Fernandez rides were not big time like those at Knotts Berry Farm, but they were good enough to sit close to a girl. They rode the Little Dipper that blasted Jerry Lee Lewis and Elvis songs, but the Caterpillar was the best bet for teens with romantic interests in mind. Halfway through that ride, a canopy automatically rose over the cars, leaving the couples to quickly initiate amours in the dark.

After the rides, the boys and girls grabbed some food and headed to the *lūʻau* tables, a much quieter area back of the food concessions, just outside the stadium. There, under the muffled light of bulbs strung from one mahogany tree to another, the gang finalized their invitations to the girls for the next night: a camp over at Kīhei and—unbeknownst to the damsels—the revenge of the creature.

After carefully toothing a candied apple, The Menace wandered off with his girlfriend with the ʻehu hair. As they passed the emergency ambulance, The Menace declared it a permanent statue. He told his date that he'd never seen the vehicle move, let alone haul off patients to the hospital. The first aid station was equally slow going. Its most serious activities were tending to the upset ʻōpū of boys who had stuffed themselves with too much cotton candy and Cokes, and the ʻōkole of old ladies poked by splinters from the grandstand seats while watching the stock car races. The Menace and his date headed toward the Commercial Building and returned with samples from all kinds of businesses including rulers, fans, and 'vote for me' cards from all the board of supervisor candidates.

Later, at the back parking lot, with the moon full over Pāʻia, The Menace and his new love traded farewell kisses in the shadow of *pandanus* trees, and another county fair faded into their memories.

Saturday evening rolled around, but the boys had not heard anything from The German. The remaining food and supplies for the camp-over filled Hi Ho's trunk, and Dishes made room in his car for The German and his monster gear. They'd meet the senior girls and the invited freshman with the ʻehu hair at Merry Andrews' house just back of St. Teresa's in Kīhei.

The boys were confused when they stopped in Wailuku at The German's house. Had he forgotten? The Bird hopped up the front stairs. "That stinker—after all the plans we made!" he chirped.

"What you talking about?" asked a voice from the car.

"It's a note. He said he had to go to Honolulu to attend his gramma's funeral."

The boys were immediately suspicious, remembering that his grandmother had died several times already to cover the German's absence excuses. Disappointed, they, nevertheless, decided to go ahead and camp out with the girls. The Creature would just have to make his appearance on another day.

Merry, Sharon Ballbarren's sister, greeted the teens at her home, introduced her new husband, and encouraged everyone to have fun. The teen squad, hauling their blankets and food for dinner and breakfast, marched out along the trail through the *kiawe* trees to the coral strewn beach.

While the girls prepared the area, and the sun began to set, Dishes, Gorge and The Menace waded out in the sea, the water so shallow at a sunset low tide that they had to trudge out a good quarter mile before their heads disappeared.

Finally, after lots of blowing and fanning, a fire was ablaze. It was followed by the banging of pots and pans in preparation for what everyone called Beany Weany. A warning was issued by the cook that the toxic beany part of the recipe could be self inflicting or murderous to a partner under a blanket beneath the stars.

With perfect timing, just as the meal was completed and the pots and pans washed and wiped, the stars appeared in the southwest sky as it turned from indigo to black. Minus the moon, the condition was ripe for a stalking monster.

Kodish resisted when Mario suggested that they all settle down and swap ghost stories, but her request was vetoed and everyone spilled out yarns, including the ones about the car with pork that stalled by the Chinese graveyard in Waiheʻe, the apparitions of the white lady of ʻĪao, and the roaming Night Marchers of Maunaʻolu. The wind whistled through the shadowless night, the girls peering about at things that weren't there, the boys with macho fronts to hide their unspoken fears. Frankly, they were not afraid of silly horror stories made up by drunks or bores but insecure with the probability that it could be a deranged escapee from the Kāne'ohe Insane Asylum. Spooked or not, the results were the same—the boys and The Menace got cheap fear hugs.

After a couple of lame attempts to scare anyone, Centa wanted the agenda changed. "Let's all take a walk down the beach; there might be scarier ghosts there," she laughed. The girls heartily agreed. The plan was then to return, restoke the fire, and commence with a marshmallow roast.

As they strolled along the sand in the dark, several came to the conclusion that this idea was perhaps not the best. The quiet was intimidating, punctuated occasionally by a howling dog in the distance, the *kiawe* trees rubbing against each other, and a rogue, "What was that?" splash out on the reef.

Suddenly, Sharon Ballbarren stopped short in her tracks, and stared out at the sea. "I thought I saw something."

"Must be your old boyfriend, Marlon Malapit, swimming from O'ahu," suggested Mario putting in his dig about his rival, a St. Louis boy who sometimes came a courtin'.

"You guys must be seeing things!" Gorge ridiculed the sighting.

"Look! Get something out there!" insisted Paula Bear, her hand dropping from Dishes' palm to point.

Hi Ho agreed. "Look, it's someone or something!" The "something" word was enough to caution the girls.

Out of the surf came a hideous looking creature. For a couple of minutes, the boys wondered if some cutthroat mass murderer had broken out of the Wailuku Jail. Then they realized that they had been took. "That son of a gun, his grandma's funeral, ha!" thought all the boys. The German had outdone himself. Aware of the situation, the boys amped the dramatics up to higher level of horror theater.

"Oh, my God, it's slimy, and it's coming towards us!" yelled Gorge.

Mario took the bait and pierced the quiet with what the gang called his girlie scream. The females took off like the start of the Indy 500.

"It's stopping!" The Menace yelled. The girls paused for a moment to look back; Sharon Ballbarren had finally snapped on her battery worn flashlight. The dismal beam increased the ambiance of fear as the soundless psycho clawed the air with his hands like *The Creature from the Black Lagoon*. The Bird stepped to the fore quickly with a clump of hardened sand and threatened the undefined thing. "Don't come closer or I'll throw this rock!"

The monster moved forward, its body's slime glistening from a smattering of illumination from the faltering flashlight. The Bird heaved the sand missile. The girls were halfway down the beach and out of range of the creature's reaction.

"Ouch!" moaned the monster. Taking advantage of the situation, each of the boys hurled their own sand grenades. Five more ouches emanated from the creature.

"This is one sensitive boogeyman!" chuckled Gorge.

"Yeah. He sounds just like that candy-ass German."

The German wanted to continue to play the role and stay in character. "Shut up, you guys! Play the game!"

"Okay, okay," they mumbled. Then all turned like Keystone Cops and raced toward the concerned girls, piercing the night with horrid guttural screams.

Merry and her husband heard the bloodcurdling wails coming from the beach and hightailed through the *kiawe* forest to see what the hell was going on. They bumped into the bevy of girls bee-lining in the opposite direction.

"What's the matter?" she yelled.

Paula Bear, between pauses trying to catch her breath, finally uttered, "There's a thing…"

"An ugly thing," added Centa. And the girls ran into the house and locked the doors.

Merry and her husband raced to the campsite to find the boys and monster rolling on the ground, celebrating another victory.

Aware of the prank, Merry queried, "German? Is that you?"

"Gotta be," added Mario.

"Great costume," noted Merry.

"It's amazing what a little gauze, tin foil, and paint can do," bragged The German.

"Promise you won't spill the beans? Tell them the thing was an old fisherman who had fallen in the surf," insisted Hi Ho.

"Mum's the word!" declared Merry.

The girls were eventually lured out of the house on the condition that Merry and her husband sleep out there with them.

As The Menace and his gang grew into adults, monsters would be the least of their worries, when considering death and taxes. Even the girl with the `ehu hair would be replaced by other girlfriends. But for now, before the blazing campfire, they burnt their marshmallows, laughed, and held hands, if only temporarily, eventually succumbing to the sweet offshore breezes of Maui, its youthful memories, and sleep.

FOR THE ROSE OF THE CHIEFS
No Ka Loke O Nā Ali`i

Upon Kamakeo's insistence, Kauikeaouli followed his older brother up the side of the old cinder cone. Of course, Kamakeo Ha`alilio was not his blood brother, but the two had been practically raised together to the point that when one started a sentence, the other ended it. Kauikeaouli always called Timothy by his Hawaiian name—Kamakeo—with the warning that Hiram Bingham, his schoolmaster, who stole his name, would then steal his land.

"I think that Reverend Bingham is sincere," huffed Timothy as they climbed up the slope.

"They're all sincere at the beginning like Cook was, until his men ripped the *koa* from our *heiau* for firewood," argued Kauikeaouli.

The two boys paused in the thicket of *hale koa* to wipe the sweat from their brows. They had forsaken the steep climb up from the oceanside of Mount Lē`ahi and replaced it with the more gradual trek up the Kapahulu side. They trudged on.

A little farther up the trail, they encountered two shirtless Hawaiian boys about their age, making their way down from the summit. As they passed, Kauikeaouli heard one of the two commoners whisper loud enough to be heard, "Keola, I think that was our new king." The other retorted, "You *pupule*! What the king doing up here?" Kauikeaouli giggled at the comments made about him.

The hike had been planned without permission from the Queen Regent, Kauikeaouli's caretaker, Ka`ahumanu. After all, the boy was now only twelve years old. His seventeen year old brother of the heart, Kamakeo Ha`alilio, who usually was on the straight and narrow path, felt that the secret escape to the top of what foreign sailors called Diamond Point would be a time to *wala`au* and clear out some of the future uncertainties that the new king was about to face.

There was not much talk. Both had been caught in the chaos with the recent return of Liholiho, Kamehameha II, who, along with his retinue, had succumbed to a contagious measles epidemic while visiting London. Having never been exposed to disease, the Hawaii party was hit extremely hard. It was a malady that not even the king could survive. He died in July, his body returned on *The Blonde* in September. Timothy shuddered. An ominous feeling of sadness came over him, the same kind of sadness he felt when he first heard of the death abroad of Liholiho. How lonely it must have been to die far from this fair land. A month had now passed, and Kauikeaouli was officially the chief of all the people but, because of his age, his stepmother, Ka`ahumanu, would run the government as Queen until Kauikeaouli was mature enough to take the mantle as Kamehameha III.

The more spriteful Kamehameha III reached the top first, shouted out his accomplishment, "*Ka Wēkiu!*", and ran like a joyfully possessed spirit along the narrow path around the parameter of the extinct volcano. Timothy raced after him but stopped halfway across the face of the crater that looked down on Waikīkī. Winded for some reason, he plopped down on a big boulder and scanned the sunny beaches seven hundred feet below, occasionally spotting an ant-like surfer braving the waves on a splinter. Timothy watched the boy in Kauikeaouli manifest himself akin to a fluttering butterfly circling a most desirous flower. The panting king finally made it back to the boulder, his skin now glistening brown against a peacock blue sky, punctuated by tumbling bleached clouds.

"Whew! That was fun! I'm glad you brought me up here, Kamakeo. I've led a sheltered life and, sadly, have seen this only from below. What a treasure we have here." Kaukeaouli squeezed up against Timothy, and the two sat speechless facing the sun being enticed by the horizon. The wind whipped contemplatively around them as both realized that a future of achievement and failure awaited this new Hawai`i, now in their hands.

"Oh, I almost forgot our toast." Kauikeaouli reached into his back pocket and pulled out a small, silver flask.

"What are you doing, Kaui?" questioned Timothy.

"This is a special occasion, the beginning of the new Hawaiian kingdom, and we must celebrate. Now, I knew that you'd object because you are a good boy. And you probably have never imbibed, but I'd like you to show me just this one time that you are human."

"I don't need to do that; I hurt and bleed like everyone else. And what's wrong about being good?" objected Timothy.

"There's nothing wrong about being good, Kamakeo. In fact, I admire that about you. There are so many people out there with bad intentions. You're the only one I can trust." Kauikeaouli looked directly into his brother's eyes. "I make this pledge to you," he continued, "that on the day I actually ascend the throne, I will appoint you my royal secretary."

"I'm honored, your highness," was the subdued response

from the older boy.

"Now, drink," demanded the boy king. "I command you this one and only time to share with me a sip of brandy. To the Chiefs!" The young heir tipped his head back and sipped then thrust the flask in a coaxing motion toward Kamakeo. The older boy took the container and re-uttered, "To the Chiefs!" The alcohol neophyte gagged as the searing liquid swirled down his throat.

"Praise the Lord!" Timothy yelled out with the fumes of conversion.

"Indeed!" echoed the king, who took another swig. He pulled a pack of sen sen from his pocket and offered it to Kamakeo. "Smothers the smell."

"Mahalo. Well, on my part, I could sit here all day, but we'd better get back before they send a search party for us," urged Timothy.

"Let's take the Waikīkī pathway down, Kamakeo," Kauikeaouli suggested. He agreed, and the two brothers-in-arms slowly descended the steep trail, the sun bronzing them in perpetuity.

Nineteen years passed, and again they sat in the copper sun, this time staring out toward Lāna'i from the verandah of Kamehameha III's Lahaina home. Reverend Richards, who would be traveling with Timothy, still had not returned from his meeting with Dr. Baldwin. It was only the two of them, the boys, now men, who had climbed up Diamond Head, some eighteen years earlier.

"Remember the pact we made at the top of Diamond Point?" asked the king. "The sun, the same orange-red."

"You've been true to your word, your highness," his royal

secretary said.

"Are you ready for your big trip, Kamakeo? I can't emphasize enough that this is the most important diplomatic mission that Hawai`i will ever take."

"If it weren't for you and the betterment of the Hawaiian Kingdom, I would rather stay at home and seep in these golden sunsets."

The young king, now in his twenties, continued his encouragement, "I wish that I could send you alone and leave Richards behind but, let's be blunt, the Americans, British, and French will look down on you because of your color and refuse to believe that a 'savage' could be as intellectually and culturally poised as you are. We've had to depend on other whites, even beyond Richards, like Mr. Simpson, to plead for us. However, once the people of these foreign lands meet you, Kamakeo, they'll be astounded that you can match and better them. I have confidence you'll succeed."

Ha`alilio mumbled humbly in reaction to the accolade. The king further insisted, "No, Kamakeo. You are our best hope for sovereignty. Too many vicious foreign *mo`o* are beginning to encircle us. Colonization is running rampant, and it's just a matter of time." He took out a pipe and stuffed it with tobacco.

Timothy reminded his childhood friend, "You'd better smoke that fast. Reverend Richards should be returning any moment. The smoke is inconsequential; what's unendurable will be his harangue about the evils of inhaling the devil's weed."

"Oh, let the man do it. It won't be the first time, and it won't be the last time he'll give me the hell-and-brimstone sermon about Christian evils."

The cook rang the dinner bell. "Well, Kamakeo, Tessie's

calling; she's made a big pot roast and a giant bowl of Waihe'e *poi* for your last land-cooked dinner until you have some enchiladas in Matzalan. All I can say is that Mr. Richards will lose out if he doesn't get back soon."

The *Shaw* left Lahaina early the next morning on the rigorous journey. First, Ha'alilio and Richards sailed across the Pacific to Matzalan, then overland by coach to Vera Cruz, another ship to New Orleans and, finally, a steamer to the United States capital. By the time they reached Washington D.C. in the cold of December 1842, they had endured five months of aching bodies, poor food, and a variety of illnesses.

It was not the first time Ha'alilio had seen snow. His early life on Hawai'i Island had afforded him the opportunity to make the trek up the sacred Mauna Kea in the middle of a Hawaiian winter to experience snowmen, snowball fights, and near frostbite. But today, the 25th seemed like another day on the calendar. It didn't seem like Christmas. To Kamehameha III's native son and diplomat for sovereignty, the celebration of the birth of Christ was, from his island experience, a peaceful day, highlighted by glorious blue skies and soft trades. It was a morning at the beach before the winds picked up, followed by an 'ōpū-filling meal of *kālua* pig, *poi*, purple yams, *kūlolo*, and *haupia*, topped off with *mele* of old days and the *wala'au* of family. All of this was in stark contrast to the drafty D.C. hotel and its smokey fireplace. The Hawaiian diplomats had to quickly devour their meal, the hotel dining room open only for a few hours so that the waiters and cooks could spend more holiday time with their families. Mr. Richards was not so concerned about the Hawaiian's eventless holiday, but more about Ha'alilio's small, but persistent cough.

"Are you all right?" asked the missionary/advisor.

"Oh, it's nothing. I'd be surprised if I didn't have a little something considering how far we've come, indoors and outdoors, hot and cold climates. I'm more concerned about the runaround we're getting from the Americans than I am about my health."

"Is this the same positive Ha'alilio that I left Hawai'i with? I remind you that John Quincy Adams was inspirational..."

"The encouragement of an ex-president is great, but it's President Tyler and the Congress that will decide our fate," Ha'alilio reminded Richards. "What got my goat was when Daniel Webster told us that he had not even read our official correspondence."

Mr. Richards insisted, "Give him credit for his honesty. The secretary of state has more demands than a small kingdom like ours."

"I'm sorry," said Timothy, "I must be tired. I'll make some hot tea and then crawl to bed and dream of the warm homeland that I miss."

The minister uttered encouragement. "Everything will seem brighter when we meet with President Tyler and his cabinet in a few days and then move on to London. The success of the coming year will mean many happy new years for Hawai'i." A yawn issued forth from Mr. Richards. "Well, I guess that's my signal to hit the sack. Good night, Timothy. Get a good sleep so that you can get rid of that cough." He walked toward the bedroom and stopped. "Oh, I almost forgot. Merry Christmas, Timothy."

"*Mele Kalikimaka* to you, Mr. Richards."

The native Hawaiian filled the teapot and placed it on the cooking shelf in the fireplace. As the water boiled, Kamakeo stared out the hotel window at the light snowfall that floated down and made the White House even whiter.

The snow that fell on the president's home turned to ice all along the East Coast as days went by. Timothy's cough had lessened, and Kamehameha III's *compadre* gained new enthusiasm and good health for their trip to England. He and Mr. Richards took the steamboat *Globe* from Washington up the coast to New Haven, Connecticut where they'd catch their ship to London.

For a long time, a battle raged in Timothy's mind over the intentions of Mr. Richards. Kauikeaouli, the king, had created in his childhood friend some doubts about these missionaries now surrounding the monarchy. He knew that conversion was their initial goal, but were there ulterior motives? He had learned to trust Reverend Bingham, but Mr. Richards was a fresh foreign face with no proven record. Kauikeaouli had reminded Kamakeo that Mr. Richards was always extremely formal; he never showed insecurity, nor let anyone into his world. His speech was measured, his correspondence without emotion or second thought. Kamehameha III concluded that the best thing that the Hawaiian rulers could do was to keep these foreigners close, on a tight leash, so to speak. It would be easier to spot any moves toward a sinister agenda. Timothy was not as wary as the king but willing to exercise caution. Hopefully, Mr. Richards would prove to be fair and honest.

No crewmember on the *Globe* paid much attention to the two travelers when they boarded the steamer that late January afternoon. The crew was quite familiar seeing gentlemen traveling with their menservants. The dinner bell rang heartily, and all the passengers filed into the dining area.

The host stopped Mr. Richards as he and Timothy moved forward. "Excuse me, sir, but your manservant cannot dine here."

Mr. Richards innocently objected, "Oh, this is not my man servant. This is Mr. Ha`alilio of the Sandwich Isles, and both of us are ambassadors to the President of the United States."

"I have eyes," argued the host. "I can distinguish white from black. Your Mr. Ha… ha… laho is of a dark, copper color. He eats at the servants' table in back."

Mr. Richards, tasting prejudice for the first time, began to object more vociferously. "This man is one of the highest and most powerful lords of the Hawaiian Kingdom!" Eyes turned towards them.

Timothy interjected to avoid confrontation, "It's okay, Mr. Richards. Perhaps you can grab me some food, and I'll eat below."

"It's not okay!" Mr. Richards insisted. He grabbed one of the crew. "Get me the Captain!" he commanded, staring back at the bothered patrons.

A grizzly white giant eventually emerged. "Good evening, sir. I'm Captain Stone. Can I be of some assistance?"

"I am Mr. Richards. Mr. Ha`alilio, here, and I are diplomats from the Hawaiian Islands to the United States, England, and France. Mr. Ha`alilio has been rejected from the dining room by your host."

The captain eyeballed Timothy from head to foot. "I'm sorry… Mr.… ?"

"Richards… Richards," seethed the missionary.

"Well, Mr. Richards, our host was merely following instructions. Manservants must eat in a designated area."

"Excuse me, Captain. You must be hard of hearing… "

"Excuse me, Mr. Richards. I think you haven't heard me

state the rules."

The usually very reserved Mr. Richards came as close to exploding that Timothy had ever seen. He suddenly stopped and, with a faux cordiality, calmly insisted, "Come, Mr. Ha`alilio." He emphasized the we. "WE will eat with the servants." Mr. Richards grabbed Timothy by the coat sleeve, and the two proudly headed to the segregated eating quarters.

Paris, June 1, 1843, was not a painted postcard summer's day. Instead of romantic blue, sable gray was reflected in the Seine; a dreary fog draped the roses in the Sun King's Tulieries Garden, the top of the Arc de Triomphe, and the imposing gargoyles of Notre Dame. In spite of the dismal atmosphere, Timothy Ha`alilio and William Richards seemed in better spirits. Five months had passed since they left the United States and, even with the snail-like hemming and hawing and lip service given by the United States government in recognizing Hawaii's sovereignty, things seemed to be faring better on the European continent, despite the distrust between England and France and their younger cousin in North America. British Secretary of State, Lord Aberdeen, French Foreign Minister, Guizot, and even King Leopold of Belgium had agreed that Hawaii should remain free. Timothy and Mr. Richards hoped to have the formal *pepa* treaty signed by the end of the year.

The cold fog was not comforting to Timothy Ha`alilio. The cough that he had picked up in Washington D.C. had returned, exasperated by the previous dampness of London and the now-chilly Paris morning. He only wished that some of the sun that spilled warmly over his Ko`olau Mountains above Honolulu would find its way to the Hotel Meurice. He muffled his cough with his handkerchief, hoping that Mr. Richards would not hear him from the adjoining bedroom. Mr. Richards was not oblivious to Ha'alilio's increasing physical deterioration and was about to suggest that Timothy be admitted to a hospital with the hope of finding the cause and cure of his ailment. The missionary had left the menu request outside the hotel room door the previous night, hoping that a hearty breakfast, lots of hot coffee, and more sleep for King Kauikeaouli's best friend would prepare him for the return trip to Hawai'i via the states.

There was a knock at the door. Mr. Richards called, "I'll get it; it's probably breakfast." The white-coated waiter placed the tray of oranges, oatmeal, biscuits, steaming coffee and the morning edition of the *Moniteur Parisien* onto the dining table. "Mr. Ha'alilio," called Mr. Richards, "come have some breakfast." The missionary, while waiting for his fellow diplomat to make his way out of the bedroom, poured himself a cup of coffee and turned to the front page of the newspaper.

Timothy heard a crash of a falling cup and a loud "oh, no" echo through the parlor. He rushed into the room.

"What's the matter, Mr. Richards?"

"I can't believe it! It happened three months ago and we only know about it now?!" continued the missionary.

"What did?" asked Timothy, trying to suppress his cough.

"Here. See for yourself!" He thrust the paper into Timothy's hands.

The native son was bewildered himself by the headline, reading it out loud: "Hawai'i has been taken possession of and occupied by British forces in the name of the Queen of England." He responded, "But this can't be!? They signed…"

Mr. Richards' immediate thought was complicity. "Two faced…" He stopped himself short of calling them illegitimate sons. "Two two-faced creatures; they must have been telling us one thing and preparing for another."

"You think the U.S. and Brits are complicit?" asked Timothy.

"What else could you imagine it is?" retorted Mr. Richards.

"Maybe it was a rogue, a lone wolf, acting on his own," urged his companion.

Mr. Richards grabbed the paper and continued. "Here. They name the culprit—a certain Paulet, whoever he is." Timothy grabbed for the coffee pot to prepare for an onslaught of coughing as Mr. Richards continued. "If I don't know a Paulet, and you don't know him, perhaps you are right. I need to get over to the French Foreign Minister's office immediately. He's probably reading the morning's headline and choking on a croissant. Perhaps he knows more." Mr. Richards groomed and dressed himself as quickly as a Parisian, grabbed a biscuit, and headed out the door. He stuck his head back in. "Oh, Timothy, when I get back, I'll be taking you to the hospital. You need to get in shape for work. We need to recheck our friends' affirmations of sovereignty before we head back to the U.S."

Timothy gave in to Mr. Richard's urgency that he see a doctor. Their limited conclusion: rheumatic pain. The doctors felt that rest and medicine was more important to combat his coughing, fatigue, and diarrhea; the latter he had kept hidden from Mr. Richards, than traipsing around the continent seeking sovereignty. Mr. Richards vowed to continue the tasks as Timothy recuperated in the Paris Hospital. They still had to return to England and the United States to finalize their recognition of sovereignty. Timothy would stay in the City of Lights for almost a month with the hope that he would eventually be given a clean bill of health. The doctors had no devices to see the damage that was building on the insides of Ha`alilio, so the Victorian physicians kept him well sedated, pain free, and regular with rectal ammonia and thirty drops a day of laudanum. The doctors weakly debated the amount of the latter drug that contained ten percent of opium, one percent morphine, and a dose of codeine. Whether or not the combination of the drugs was lethal was not heavily considered. All the doctors did agree, however, that it was the quickest avenue of improvement. Thankfully, Timothy improved, if only temporarily, and he and Mr. Richards arrived in London on July 18.

Work was still to be done. Timothy continued to rest in London, as Mr. Richards shuttled back and forth between England and France and finally produced a document from the two world powers recognizing Hawaiian independence.

With time, Ha`alilio seemed to have made a remarkable recovery, and he and Mr. Richards set sail on the *Britannia* for America on May 4, 1844. The missionary suggested that they forgo, because of Timothy's illness, the original U.S. itinerary that they had created before they left Hawai`i as part of the last leg of their trip abroad. But after the encouragement they received from the new Secretary of State, John C. Calhoun, Timothy seemed instilled with new life and insisted that he and Mr. Richards see some of the great American cities in a loop that started at Wheeling and then moved on to Pittsburgh, Cleveland, and Buffalo, with stops at Niagara Falls, then onto Syracuse and Albany with a sail down the Hudson to New York.

Mr. Richards had fallen asleep in his chair next to Timothy's bed at Massachusetts General but was awakened by talking in the dark. The companion of Ha`alilio instinctively grabbed his pocket watch. It was 2:00 a.m. He could again hear the ailing Hawaiian. The patient was unaware, from the intensity of the medicinal drugs, that Mr. Richards was present. The loop of the American cities had taken its toll, and Timothy had relapsed into an even more intense wasting.

"I'm sorry, your majesty," called Timothy into the darkness. "I wish I was stronger to pursue our mission with more vigor." Mr. Richards presumed that Timothy was hallucinating, seeing himself before Kamehameha III reporting on his diplomatic journey. Suddenly, his attempt at breathing was almost convulsive as he tried to swallow any bit of air. Three doctors—Jackson, Hale, and Bigelow—had been assigned to assist the ailing visitor from the Sandwich Islands and had come to the conclusion that a section of his lung had deteriorated. In addition, his pulse had been so erratic that the physicians finally stopped taking it.

With a heave of his chest, Ha`alilio called out in the night, "Father, forgive me; I know not what I do." Mr. Richards, the former missionary, was moved by the litany of trivial sins that followed from the mouth of a near saint: "I'm sorry, mother, for not loving you more. Bless me, oh chiefs, for not giving you my all. My amends to you, Mr. Richards, for my doubts about success."

Timothy attempted another deep breath, this one so painful that he cried out. Mr. Richards naturally moved toward the bed, grabbed the sick ambassador's hand and, consciously, for the first time, let sensuousness be joined with compassion. He stroked Timothy's forehead between the valleys of his fingers. In the little autumn moonlight that spilled into the hospital room, Richards saw tears of human suffering flow down Timothy's wan face.

"Don't cry," cracked Mr. Richards' saddened voice.

After a slight pause, Timothy managed to say, "I am not crying for me. I'm crying for you." With the more sudden thought that this might be his last night on Earth, he continued, "Not my will but Thine be done."

That was the last thing Mr. Richards remembered that night.

"You're going to get a stiff neck sleeping that way." Mr. Richards was awakened by the admonition, and lifted his head off the leg of the patient.

"Oh, I'm sorry, Timothy, I seemed to have dozed off." The assisting friend rubbed the morning from his eyes, happy to see that the final words of a dying man the night before had not been not realized.

Dr. Jackson made his way into the room. "Mr. Ha`alilio, are you up for breakfast? I made my way through the market place last night and came upon a couple of pineapples and mangoes from Spain and dropped them off with your cook. I thought that some familiar tropical fruit would compliment this morning's show of sunshine and make you feel a little better." A faint but genuine smile formed. However, the mere attempt of waking up was in itself too strenuous, so Timothy dozed off again.

"Come, Mr. Richards. I need to talk to you," urged Dr. Jackson.

Mr. Richards knew well enough what this speech would be about—one that he hoped never would come. He braced himself for the doctor's words.

"It's time, Mr. Richards. Did he leave a last will and testimony?"

"He did. I've gone out and shopped for specific cloths for his mother, coats and hats for his king; his steamer trunk with all his worldly belongings he has left for the chiefs."

"Are you still intent on taking him home?" asked the doctor.

"I know that you are against it, but that has been his consistent demand—that he see his homeland once again. I've made arrangements for us to leave on the *Montreal* on November 18."

Doctor Jackson understood. "He can probably make it to the ship next week, but the probability is that he will not make it all the way."

"I will not bury him at sea, so do you have any suggestions how we may preserve the body, so that he can have the proper burial in Honolulu?"

"Let me talk to the other doctors, Mr. Richards. We'll meet again tomorrow. Now, I suggest you get some sleep. We don't want you ill. There's much more work to do until you reach the Sandwich Isles."

It would take months to get to Hawai'i; both Mr. Richards and Timothy were expected to sail into Honolulu about the third week of March, some seventy plus days after departure from Boston. Both realized that their expectations had been set very high.

It was a cold November 18 when the thin and very sickly Ha'alilio was moved onto the *Montreal* by stretcher and placed down in one of the more comfortable cabins. Snuck on board and out of his sight was a lead coffin filled with alcohol for the inevitable.

Timothy was wracked with pain, praying with or without Mr. Richards, with faith that his life was in the hands of the Lord. He awoke on the third of December before sunrise and pounded on the wall for Mr. Richards, asleep in the next cabin. Mr. Richards grabbed his robe and hurried into Ha`alilio's berth.

"What's the matter, Timothy?" was Richards' concern.

"Mr. Richards, today is the day we go on deck," said Timothy with full intent. Mr. Richards was taken aback by the clarity and confidence in Ha`alilio's voice. But, at the same time, he was concerned about the unusual demand.

"Right now?"

"Yes, so we can witness the rising of the sun," added the sick man.

"Let me get into some warmer clothing and grab a few deck hands to help carry you up there." Although Mr. Richards was at the point of exhaustion from the many months of assisting his friend, he cast aside personal needs to help a man whose days were numbered.

Within fifteen minutes, Timothy had been borne by stretcher to the deck. He requested, "Mr. Richards, can you take me starboard?"

"For any particular reason, Timothy?"

"I want to face west; I want to face my homeland."

"As you say, Timothy," said Mr. Richards.

The missionary and the deck hands hoisted the dying man, moved him starboard, and set him up in a comfortable position near the rail. He thanked the deck hands with aloha then encouraged them to return to their work.

The sun was now rising above the Atlantic, the ship just short of slipping past the Carolinas. The back of Hawaii's favorite son was now framed by the golden rays that shone down on the East Coast, the same rays that warmed the land of his chiefs. The temporary burst of energy that got him on deck seemed suddenly to wane.

"If you look good, Mr. Richards, you can see it," squinted Timothy.

"See what, Timothy?"

"My home, Mr. Richards, my home. I see Mother pacing at the porch, waiting. She's prepared *mahi* and *poi*. Soon we'll be talking about old times."

"I'm sure she's excited that she'll see her son soon," Mr. Richards added.

"I can smell it, Mr. Richards—the air after the sun follows the Puanaiea rain; the joy after the sorrow. I can hear it—the waves breaking at Waikīkī, and the abandon of my youth. I can feel it—the last rays of Lahaina at dusk painting my face with the warmth and security of simple times."

Mr. Richards gazed into Timothy's eyes; they seemed to glow and affirm that he really was there, not only envisioning Honolulu and O'ahu but all the islands that he had toured with Kauikeaouli.

Weakly, he uttered, "Did I do well for my chiefs, Mr. Richards?"

Mr. Richards whispered back, "You have done well, Timothy. You have achieved your mission. Sovereignty is ours."

Timothy grabbed Mr. Richards' hand one last time.

Like many times on their trip, communications came late, way after the event. Prior to Haalilo's death Mr. Richards had sent a letter of their estimated date of arrival on a ship that left Boston for Honolulu, before the departure of the *Montreal*.

Smaller ships had spotted the returning vessel near the islands on the third week of March, so Hawaiians began to gather early on March 21—Ha'alilio and Richards' due date. Chiefs and commoners alike swarmed Honolulu Harbor, waving flags that Ha'alilio himself had designed, emblazoned on the them the words that he had given his life for: *Ua Mau Ke Ea o Ka 'Āina I Ka Pono*—The Life of the Land is Preserved in Righteousness. The arms of the populace dangled *lei*, several bands gathered to strike up songs of welcome, and gleeful children strained their eyes out toward Diamond Point. Gazing out to Mount Lē'ahi, as well, was Timothy's boyhood companion, King Kauikeaouli. The natural landmark triggered the memory of the day when he and his mentor climbed the walls of the ancient caldera, and when he and Kamakeo sat at its edge, bronzed perpetually by the setting sun. The king and his people were unaware that their tears of joy would shortly turn to tears of sadness.

The crowd's chatter rose to a crescendo as the ship loomed larger.

Timothy Ha'alilio's wish had come true. He was now home. He had returned to the 'Rose of His Chiefs'—Hawai'i.

ON THE WINGS OF BLUEBIRDS
I Nā Hulu ʻEkekeu o Nā Manu Uli

Word had gotten out even before the announcement hit the *Maui News*. Kids from Happy Valley and Kahului flooded the YMCA grounds, flocked around the Wailuku Pool in anticipation of the arrival of The Duke, their feet dipped in the placid, virgin surface like Polynesian flamingos. Butch had anticipated the delirium of Duke fans, and even though he lived merely a mango's throw from his front porch to the Wailuku Pool, Butch had hung out near the new high dive board since the lifeguard had flung open the new gate at 7:30 a.m. He looked out at the new extended pool; the old one had been expanded and deepened over the last few months, and it was only fitting that Hawaii's greatest Olympian had been chosen to dedicate the new swim center.

For the last seventeen years, the Alexander Sports Complex in Wailuku had been the hangout for Butch and his brothers, whether in the pool, in the gym or on the outdoor courts. He would have even played tennis among the rich if he could afford to buy a racket. But, today would not be just another day at the center. Someone famous was moseying into his territory, and it was the Sheriff of Honolulu, Duke Kahanamoku.

A crowd had even gathered along Wells Street, the sudden

increase of chatter and shouts signaling the approach of the guest star. A black 1938 Ford made its way toward the pool and pulled up in front of the YMCA building. Butch spotted the smiling Duke peering out the window at him and all the future swimmers and surfers.

Another blast of "Hooray!" was bellowed forth by the crowd. It was an added guest, Butch thought, from the joyful glee. He couldn't believe it! Another celebrity emerged from the car. It was Flash Gordon himself!—Buster Crabbe! Butch was not ignorant about Buster's accomplishments in the swim world. His mom seemed to well up in pride when she talked about Buster Crabbe, the Punahou graduate, who occasionally popped up on Maui to visit relatives. He had taken the celebrity status gained from swimming to a wider popularity in the movies. He was Flash Gordon and Tarzan all rolled into one. To Butch, the two swimmers emitted that Hollywood glow as they moved near the area where he sat.

"Could we have your attention, everyone?" shouted the head lifeguard. "I'd like to introduce the Chairman of the Board of Supervisors, Mr. Harold Rice, who will introduce our special guests." The politician spilled forth a seemingly endless history of Maui pools and the bloated courage it took to build them. The blabbering of the elected official, along with the increasingly warming spring sun, tested the patience of anxious little boys and the endurance of restless teens. The neighborhood kids merely wanted to see the Duke and Tarzan the Fearless swim. Finally, the homily ended with, "Here to christen our new pool are Duke Kahanamoku and Buster Crabbe!"

The two pulled off their shirts to reveal their swimmer physiques, took a step up on the deep end wall, and plunged into the blue pool. A cheer poured up into ʻĪao Valley as the two local swimmers comically prevented each other from making it to the wall at the shallow end. They both went into mocked slow motion for the last few yards, each trying to get there at the same time for a gratuitous tie.

As soon as they touched the wall, a whistle was blown and a hundred kids bombarded the newly dedicated pool, creating a furious frenzy of delirious splashing, joined in by the two aquatic legends. Eventually, the two slipped away and into dry pairs of trunks and settled in an area poolside to "talkstory" with the kids. Another whistle blew followed by an announcement that there would be a question and answer session with The Duke and Flash Gordon on the grassy knoll under the royal palms.

"Ask our guests any questions you want," announced the head lifeguard. Butch was familiar with how local kids usually went into their quiet mode when solicited for questions; they had to be prodded out of their shyness, and so it was on this day under Maui skies. Finally, after an uncomfortable silence, Butch decided to ask the first question.

"Mr. Kahanamoku, can you tell us what it was like to break the Olympic record?" The Duke had been asked the question many times, and he answered it without reservation, ending the retelling of the event, as he usually did, by mentioning that he had been beat by "that guy who swings from trees".

"Hey, don't give me stink eye. It's that other Tarzan—that Weismuller feller," corrected Buster in defense of the stares directed toward the antagonist to Ming the Merciless.

"How does it feel to be a hero in the Olympics?" asked little Del DeRego seated in the shadows of the great swimmers.

Buster Crabbe rescued the question from a Duke who he knew would never admit to being a hero. He turned the question around to the little neighborhood boy. "What is a hero, son?"

Little Del looked up, paused, "Somebody that helps somebody, that saves them, you know, like Superman."

"And do you think Duke helped or saved someone when he swam the fastest in the world?"

The future lawyer loved The Ape Man's line of questioning. "No." He paused. "Then, he's not a hero?" reclaimed the boy.

"You said a hero was someone who saved another. Duke is a hero not because he won gold medals in Stockholm, Antwerp and Paris. He is a hero because he actually saved people. Here's what happened:

Duke was in Hollywood. His Olympic fame was a door opener to show biz. He and a couple of his movie friends were spending a day at Corona Del Mar at Newport Beach, just south of Los Angeles."

Buster turned to Duke to encourage him to tell the story in his own words. "Come on, Duke, tell the kids what exactly happened. You know, in your own way."

Ordinarily, the rather shy Duke would have avoided tooting his own horn, but Buster had put him on the spot and so, on second thought, the Father of Surfing began his version, feeling that the story might, if for any other reason, result in a future life being saved.

"The day started as any other, the warm California sun beating down on a calm sea. I was in Hollywood making movies. Jimmy Spencer and some of the cast members from my yet to be released pictures, *The Pony Express* and *Lord Jim*, were celebrating my first film effort, *Adventure*, Jack London's story directed by the great Victor Fleming. Luckily, I had brought along my board. I went everywhere with that thing. Some fib that I take it to bed with me so I can surf in my dreams. A couple of boards had been stashed at the bathhouse at the end of the beach with the thought that they might be used to rescue someone, someday. Little did we know that it would be that very morning. We were going to give our actress dates a crash course in the art of *he'e nalu* before lunch. No sooner were the blankets spread and the lunch provided by the girls evaluated as *'ono* was I distracted. I turned to notice the crashing of waves around the pier; the rise of the breakers was certainly sudden. My instincts pointed my attention to a boat seeming to have a hard time making it into safe harbor. Each couple of yards forward was offset by the buffeting of barn size walls of water. I borrowed a pair of binoculars from a couple picnicking nearby and noted the vessel's name – *The Thelma*, a charter fishing boat. I also spied the anguish on the faces of the tourist fishermen as they clung, white knuckled, to the guardrail. It did not look good. The swells grew larger and as threatening as a red flag day at Makapu'u. Suddenly, like a speeding locomotive, a mountainous wave cascaded down on *The Thelma,* turning her over, dumping crew and tourist fishermen into the maelstrom.

I pitied the poor people who had never learned to swim. I could imagine the fear they had at the thought of losing their lives, a fear that I had replaced with respect a long time ago, an anxiety that still sometimes plagues even a sea veteran like me. It was obvious that I had to do what I had to do. I grabbed the board and headed out into the chaos. I shouted out to my shocked friends, 'Jimmy, guys! Go get the boards at the bathhouse! Follow me out!' I pleaded with the Lord that I wanted to save all but could only do so much with this surfboard. 'Oh, give me back those Olympic arms for a few minutes,' I prayed.

It was hard to focus on anything: people, debris, the loose ship crashing into the pier. I ignored the peril to my life and grabbed the body of a flailing victim. I must say that he was surprised to see a brown man demanding that he slide on the board but assented to the mere joy of being saved. In the midst of all the heartbreak was humor. Spitting water between words, a hopeful man yelled out, 'Going my way?' 'Grab the back of the board!' I shouted. I paddled the first two victims to shallower water where they were ushered to dry land by the girls and some other good Samaritans. I turned immediately and thrust back out to the state of confusion. Where the heck was Jimmy and the guys with the other surfboards? I could only do so much, but I would have to bring in as many as could pile onto the board. I then saw a sight for sore eyes! A Coast Guard boat appeared, trying to barge its way into the area. It would not be easy. The cutter became entangled, like *The Thelma*, under a Niagara Falls of pounding surf. I spotted another man who had toppled overboard pleading loudly, 'Help. I can't swim. I'm getting weaker!'

    I paddled over to silence the beggar and calm the other bobbing bodies. 'Brudda, relax. I've come for you,' I said. The man deliriously grabbed at the board, forcing the *papa he'e nalu* and me to overturn into the boiling surf. I pleaded calmly again. 'It's okay, my friend. You are saved.' The man took a deep breath as I heaved him onto the board, his tears commingling with the salt water splashes. He pleaded 'My brother… he's back there!' I turned to see his now weakened sibling trying to shed his bulky fishing jacket. I paddled over, helped him tear the extra weight from his body, and slopped him on board. The two jabbered like mynah birds the whole way in; I was oblivious to what they actually said; my concern was with the remaining floaters. I grew increasingly frustrated. I could not continue this type of *manini* rescues when scores were in the water. I had to face the fact that some would sadly drown.

Luckily, Jimmy and the other males had finally found and pulled their stored surfboards from the bathhouse and were making their way out. On the third trip out, I became more conscious of those who had given up or had consumed huge quantities of water, their bodies dangling freely like puppets in the swells, slowly sinking. I didn't know that seventeen had indeed perished, my mind set on the catastrophe at hand. My job now was to save those hungry to live. I had to take back more. I would try three on the next trip. Fortunately, I spotted the lucky one just yards from me, crying out loud that he was going to die, his two friends, hiding their personal fears by comforting him, while being barraged by the pounding waves. They heaved the hysterical fishing buddy onto the *papa he'e nalu* as I got close. Death grips clutched the board as I headed to shore. I was followed in by Jimmy and the other less experienced surfers; happily, they had been able to save four. I turned around after dislodging the victims to find before me a bodiless surf. The battered Coast Guard cutter and some helpful seamen had pulled the remaining survivors to safety. The scene finally looked hopeful, but the reality was that many had drowned and had sunk to their watery graves. The task of saving humans was an incomparable challenge to dragging dead bodies from the bottom and having their weeping kin identify their remains."

The Duke paused for a moment, aligning his thoughts not about his duty out of necessity, but about swimming and survival in the lives of his youthful audience.

"What does this have to with all you kids here? Well, the value of swimming at this point in your life is the joy of catching a wave, the fun of splashing and diving, and the peace of floating under a blue sky. But someday, and I hope it will never come, you will realize the value of swimming and survival—not only your survival but the survival of others."

"Hey, kids, do you mind if I ask Mr. Kahanamoku a question?" asked Buster. They responded positively to Dale Arden's protector.

"Hey, Duke, I've always heard about the famous bluebirds and heard that you rode one for a mile."

Duke leaned over to little Del DeRego. "Do you know what Flash is talking about?" Little Del shook his head from side to side.

"Well, it's a wave, maybe several waves, that come barreling across the Pacific, probably due to an earthquake. They are huge, usually over thirty feet. Now, most surfers would be happy to surf a distance of two to three hundred feet, and get really delirious at five hundred. But can you imagine a wave that keeps on going? That's what a bluebird is, and it may appear only once in a lifetime."

"Tell us about it!" demanded little Del.

"Well, son. It was 1917, about twenty years ago. I was with my friend, Dad Center, bored, bobbing on a very glassy sea at Kalāhuewehe, way out, about five hundred yards off of Castle Point. Surfers and ship captains called it Castle Point because of a huge medieval mansion that sat out on the bluff. We were part of the dawn patrol—early morning surfers. The sun had been up for an hour. Suddenly, I thought I heard the sound of a locomotive as if it was making its way across the Moloka'i Channel. But it wasn't no train. It was a series of huge waves—and they were headed toward us. Dad Center and I felt the first watery mammoth slide under our *koa* boards. We issued a "whoa" in unison at the unusual heave. I was lucky to have the sixteen footer with me; these were the kinds of waves that demanded the biggest stick. I was determined to take the next one—aware that one slip, one wrong decision, would result in the equivalency of a huge building crashing down on me.

I took the behemoth, and off I went, careening down its face, the water gushing so fast past my sides that it mocked Gatling gun fire. Most good surfers could end up at Elk's, but this wave wasn't stopping. Public Baths was the second possible destination, so on I rode, taming the wild mustang. Suddenly, two other waves joined the one I was riding on, and gave me a further boost. I knew I could now make it to Queen's, and perhaps beyond, at this pace. The watery express train did just that; the remaining energy zipped me a thousand feet past Cunha's to Queen's before it finally pooped out."

"What every surfer dreams of at night," commented Buster. Applause from a hundred little hands filled the air. The head lifeguard announced that after autographs, Duke would have to get back to his job as sheriff and Buster blast back to the Planet Mongo. Butch, Little Del and the kids of the neighborhood lined up to get their swim shorts, fins, or soaked programs autographed to commemorate the day when the best in the world had graced their pool.

Years later, when Butch would pull a swimmer from the bottom of a California pool, he would recall the day when Duke looked into his eyes and told his story about the people he saved at Corona Del Mar, and about the time Paoa flew on the wings of bluebirds.

NOTES ON SHORT STORIES

I WALKED WITH THE NIGHT MARCHERS

Everyone is curious about the occult, and nothing stirs more interest in locals than experiences of ghosts, specifically night marchers. Three locally popular movies about night marchers were made by Big Island filmmakers, Blake and Brent Cousins, and some are familiar with Rap Replinger's comedy bit about the hotel host trying to downplay the fact that night marchers walk through the hotel property. Ghosts have different reasons for appearances, and this is also true of night marchers. One reason, and the one that is chosen for this story, is to relive a lost battle with the intent to win this time. Sadly, the warriors are ignorant that the desire can never be fulfilled. I picked one of the more famous battles for the ghosts to relive—the first battle for Maui against Kahekili by Big Island Ali`i, Kalaniopu`u and Kamehameha the Great. Several decades ago, workers, constructing the Waikapū golf course that now sits in the 1775 battle path, claim that strange things happened including machinery that stopped for no reason, and the moving of giant boulders overnight. The story significantly takes place on that golf course on the thirteenth hole.

A DAY AT THE PALACE / A NIGHT AT THE OPERA

Film buffs are aware of the second half of the title of this piece as a film with the Marx Brothers, and that's what I set out to do with this story—write a fairly quick-moving comedy, full of interruptions and silliness. Most stories of the Hawaiian monarchy are portrayed with gravitas. I wanted to depict the members of the royalty in the opposite vein, at a moment when they were warm and funny as they were portrayed in some scenes from my play, *Children of the Turning Tide*. During my research of the period, I became aware that Liliuokalani had composed an opera. For many years, researchers thought that the libretto and songs gathered up after the queen had passed away had been written by another artist because the author's name appeared on the documents as Madame Aorena. After a handwriting analysis of the script, researchers came to the conclusion that the light comedy in the vein of Gilbert and Sullivan was indeed penned by Liliuokalani under the European sounding pseudonym. In this story everyone is trying, with some difficulty, to achieve something: Liliuokalani (Lydia) is looking for inspiration for the opera, David (Kalākaua) is attempting to leave on his round-the-world trip, Miriam (Likelike) and Bernice (Pauahi Bishop) are nervously preparing for their operatic debut in *H.M.S. Pinafore*, and Annis Montague (Cooke), now a renowned diva, is returning home to perform some fundraising concerts. Everyone's reacting to a new invention called the telephone, and there's a mongoose on the loose in the midst of the renovation of ʻIolani Palace.

THE FIRES OF PU'UO'UMI

Father Damien was canonized in 2009, and Hawaii's citizens welled up in pride at the sanctification of one of their sons. The Belgian priest had indeed earned his status as one of us when he dedicated his life to the leprosy patients of Kalaupapa, eventually contracting and dying from the disease. My curiosity posed the question: Under what circumstances would a man volunteer for a fatal job? The motivation would have to have occurred prior to Moloka`i. Some do not realize that before to his commitment to the Friendly Isle, Father Damien (Kamiano) served for a number of years in Puna and then eight years at Waiāpuka, both located on the Big Island of Hawai`i. My belief is that he encountered someone there who was inflicted with Hansen's disease, and that a personal relationship inspired his call to Kalaupapa. I failed to find the smoking gun (specific names), but in a letter to Bishop Maigret from Kohala, Damien urged the diocese to do something about the scourge that was running rampant on the island. I have attempted in the story to give a face and a soul to the undocumented life of a leper that Damien probably tended to and bonded with. The story's title refers to the upland cooking fires of the outcasts and the highest ridge above Waiāpuka named after `Umi, the mightiest ali`i before Kamehameha the Great.

THE BIG L

While doing research for my previous book, *Under Maui Skies and Other Stories*, I was reacquainted with the robbery of the Pāʻia Bank of Hawaiʻi. I was more familiar with the robbery by the policeman in the ʻ50s, but vaguely knowledgeable about the bank robbery at the same site in 1938—Maui's first. There were only a few basic newspaper accounts of the ʻ30s incident but, with the help of some old timers, I gathered personal versions and additions. The rest of the story had to be filled in. Who were these two robbers? Why did they rob the bank? Was there any connection to the nationwide crime wave (e.g. Dillinger)? What was their plan? Did it work? Where did they hide the money? How did they get caught? These were the questions that my experience and imagination would answer in a narrative form. The silliness of the two bank robbers naturally steered the story toward comedy. Half the fun of writing the piece was playing with pidgin again and re-creating Lahaina and other Maui locales of the 30s. The references to Maui establishments like the Liberty Restaurant, the Banyan Inn and the Queen Theater should bring back memories to old timers and history buffs. All those establishments are now gone, except one. The original bank building in Pāʻia, where the first of multiple robberies occurred, still sits, though now abandoned, just off the sidewalk on Baldwin Avenue.

THE TRAIL TO MĀNĀ

Under Maui Skies, my short story from the book of the same name, is a tale about a simple Maui cowboy hired by the sheriff to keep an eye on an opium smuggler named Albert Devil. I wanted to set that turn-of-the-century story against a big event happening in town to increase the reader's pity for the poor roper. I ran across the famous event in Hawaiian history, and it became the celebration that Ramon would miss—the dance and party to hail Parker Ranch cowboy, Ikua Purdy. Purdy, Archie Ka`aua, and Jack Low had just broken the world record in roping at the National Rodeo Championship in Cheyenne, Wyoming and were touring the islands. My interest in this event spurred me to dig into the details of it, including an afternoon talk story at the `Ulupalakua ranch of Nancy Purdy, the widow of Ikua's late son, Dan. The dynamism of the national win seemed to lead back to Eben Low, the financial sponsor of the men's trip to Waiomina (Wyoming in Hawaiian). I wanted to make the connection between Eben and Ikua and show how a negative, the loss of Low's hand, led to a positive, the first *paniolo* to win a national rodeo title. My working title for a while was "The Day Eben Low Lost His Hand and Ikua Purdy Won the National Rodeo Championship". With little detail about their journey, I blended a train trip I took when I was nineteen from San Francisco to Cheyenne on the Union Pacific, the same train route of the traveling Hawaiians. One shocking discovery during research was the racist pre-rodeo headlines of the Wyoming newspapers. After the men came in first, third, and sixth, the papers replaced their prejudiced headlines with more congratulatory ones. Recently, both

Waimea and Cheyenne celebrated the 100th anniversary of Ikua, Archie, and Jack's triumph. Ikua is buried in a simple grave in ʻUlupalakua, near the ranch that he worked on until his death, July 4, 1945.

THE TEENAGE CREATURE FROM THE BLACK LAGOON

My teenage years on Maui in the 1960s were both similar and different from my mainland peers. As the opening scene shows, kids at matinees here and there made a lot of noise and threw popcorn at the ushers. But add some local color like sucked dry crackseed bag missiles at the King Theater and chow fun at the Maui County Fair and you'll see the cultural differences between us and our continental counterparts. I again revisit my teenage friends as I did in my play `Ili `Ili and my short story, "Luahinepi`i", in *Under Maui Skies and Other Stories*. I blended a teenage love story with the nostalgia of three events—a typical island football game, the Maui County Fair, and a local style beach camp-out complete with guest monster. I wasn't heavily concentrating on plot in this short story, merely exploring the awkwardness and demands of first loves and, simultaneously, soaking in Maui's memorable past.

FOR THE ROSE OF THE CHIEFS

Val and Ollie Dukelow and Laurel Douglass and Guy Gaumont made me aware of Ha`alilio, and the assignment by Kauikeaouli, Kamehameha III, in the mid-1800s, to bring back a *pepa* of agreement that stated that the major powers had granted Hawai`i its sovereignty, in spite of past and continuing colonization efforts by England, France, and the United States. The research challenge was enormous, but, thankfully, the Dukelows and Seeti Douglass had gathered two volumes of documents, including ship itineraries, various reports, and letters. Because Timothy Ha`alilio and Kauikeaouli were close confidants from boyhood, I created the opening scene of the two climbing Diamond Head in their youth, then jumped to the day before Kamakeo (Timothy) headed off to the United States with Mr. Richards. This is the same Mr. Richards who was the spiritual thorn in the side of both Kauikeaouli and his sister, Princess Nahi`ena`ena, in my short story, "The Cruel Sun", from *Under Maui Skies and Other Stories*. From the onset, I realized that this was indeed a tragedy, a story of triumph and defeat, life and death. Whether Ha`alilio, Hawaii's gifted and honored child, was "removed from the scene" or merely suffered from primitive Victorian health care and an overdose of prescribed drugs, we learned of the integrity of this most saintly character, and the fact that Hawai`i did get its sovereignty... until. The Rose in the title, *For the Rose of the Chiefs,* represents the homeland of the ali`i—Hawai`i.

ON THE WINGS OF BLUEBIRDS

I always admired Duke Kahanamoku and became even more enamored when I researched him for my play *Steamer Days: The View from Aloha Tower*. In fact, some day I'd like to write a play solely about him. Recently, I fell in love with Nathan Kurosawa's film, *The Ride*, and felt more compelled to retell one of Duke's great experiences. One of the fascinating stories was his saving of near drowning victims of a sinking boat near Newport Beach, California. The Roaring 20s, a California beach, the movies and the first serious use of surfboards for lifesaving on the mainland combine for the elements of a colorful tale. The story is introduced by way of the Wailuku Pool where, like my father, I learned to swim, and where Duke Kahanamoku and Buster Crabbe came to inaugurate the improved facility in 1936.

KAONA
AND OTHER MELE

KE KOHOLĀ

Cheery hearted traveler
Maui's warm waters welcome
Your permanent homecoming
O powerful swimmer
Gifted flippers, fluke
Na Huila of the sea
O giant of gentility
Sing your magic songs
A *mele* of new and earned life
In harmony
With playful porpoise now
With all ancestors joined
Splashes heard in the night
It is the spirit of largeness
It is the whisper of finesse
In the ocean of imagination.

na huila – wheels
mele – song

KA ULUA

All creatures of the sea
Pay homage to the *ulua*
Commoner as *pāpio*
Royalty as elders,
Lustrous kingfish
Independent sojourner
Or sparkling splinter in an undersea cloud
The evasive one grows
His security preserved in the maze of lava reef
Or in shadow of shark or seal
Pursued pelagic
Or pursuer of `oama and flying fish into the shallows
Governed by the silver moon
Sprinkling the surface of a midnight lagoon.

pāpio - another name for ulua in young stage
pelagic - deep water fish
`oama - young of the weke, goatfish

KA ʻULA ʻULA

O Gem of the Sea
Ruby of the deep
Celebrating the journey of twelve moons
O *ʻUla ʻUla o Hawaiʻi Nei*
O Onaga o ʻIāpana
Your red dorsal joins sea to sky
How deep is the plunge
To the rocky bottoms
Where the prize thrives among a universe of starfish
Shunner of burnt flesh
He retreats the summer in hibernation
To grow and paint the sea pink in winter
The tint of the *Lokelani*

ʻula ʻula - red
onaga o ʻIāpana - Japanese name
lokelani - Maui rose

KA MOI

Kaupō is dark now
When the dawn breaks on the eastern sea
The chop will give way to a brief calm
Hurry to the *ko`a*, the special feeding spot
Come view the sacred *moi*
Do not take the adults
It is only for the *`ōpū* of the *ali`i*
Kapū to the *keiki*
Ignorant of the moon phases
I spot the red-eyed one
It is a four pounder
One that can be generously shared with the *ali`i* and me.

Kaupō - East Maui village
ko`a - where fish gather
`ōpū - stomach
ali`i - chief
kapū - forbidden
keiki - child

KE KŌLEA

The singing snails announce
A deity is among us
Koleamoku is a flyer
Who returns to feed in the high grass
Or Kōlea Kai Piha, along the shore
O message bearer to the *ali`i*
Do not circle my home
Instead, *E ai kākou!*
Let us eat, celebrate, before you leave
The Wandering Tattler, your travel companion
Brags of your golden Plover feathers
Tuusiik! Tuusiik! lures `Ālaka
Time to leave your narrow shoreline
The tide has risen
Kūnou! Kūnou!
Bobbing your noddy
A prelude to flight.

singing snails - tree snails that make sounds
Tuusiik! the word given to bobbing by Alaskan natives
`Ālaka - Alaska
Kūnou! - the word given to bobbing by Hawaiian natives
noddy - head

KE KALO

The peace of the flowing *wai* of the *lo`i*
The *kalo* stands rooted in the soil of its ancestors
The native of generations
O big leaved fish of the land
No bones this food for *keiki*
Content this *kalo* in his own place
Listen to the whispers, the winds of Waihe`e
The voices of the bitter purple plum branches
The twirling of the *kukui* leaves, dark, light
The journey is long, the *kalo* light
O simple sustenance
Now is *Welo*, the time for planting
The rains are ripe
The mature *kalo*
An offering as precious as *pua`a*
At Kealakaihonua at the sea
And to your back the misty Mauna Alani.

wai - water
lo`i - kalo patch
kalo - taro root
keiki - child
Waihe`e - village, North Maui
kukui - candlenut tree
Welo - month of lunar calendar
pua`a - pig/pork
Kealakaihonua - Waihe`e heiau
Mauna Alani - mountain above Waihe`e

KE KOA

Kilakila e ke koa
Voices brag of your strength
Your seed issued in the bosom of Kāne
Pulled taut like the reclining coconut trees of Kalapana
You frolicked at Kalehua
A dream drifting to Kailua
Then off to the land of Nā Wai Ēha
Rooted between *nā pali* o Kapalehua a A`alaloa
Your towering branches shield, protect all under its shade
In the seer of summer, the whips of winter
Your scattered seeds are later barks imagined
Ke koa's life does not end in the *waikele*
The fallen tree is not *make*'
He is shaped into a voyager
Heading for that island that appears in the mist
Similar to the beauty of those islands he was rooted in
Except now, a *moku* without strife
He is greeted by those waiting for him with the sweet *hā* of love.

kilakila - majestic
Kāne - god of Creation and Light
Kalapana - village/land section, Puna, Big Island
Kalehua - area famous for surfing. Puna, Big Island
Nā Wai Ēha - the four streams
pali - cliffs
waikele - forest
make - dead
moku - island
hā - breath

KA UA KEA O HĀNA

O Land of Ka'ahumanu, of Pi'ilani, of the *maka'āinana*
Come climb the hill, Kā'uiki calls, for one last time
Come listen to the rain on the *'awapuhi ke'oke'o*
Drip rhythmically, and create perfume for angels
The Son of Ka'eokulani pierces the banana leaf
Not the sky, not with spear, but song
O humble rain, nature's baptism, you refresh anew
Come mix with the *'ehu kai*, wafting from the Bay
The *Mālualua* will carry you to cool Hāmoa
The strings in my heart, slacken with your kindness
Echo the songs of ancestors
O Wānanalua is the land
O Punahoa is the pond
O Kā'uiki is the hill
O Ka Ua Kea of Hāna is the *mele*
The tears fall, the clouds weep
But tomorrow *mālie* Hāna
For Kaihuokala will be clearly seen
Every time *aokū* gather over Pu'uki'i
And drops strum its *niu*
Remember Ka Ua Kea o Hāna.

Glossary: ua kea (white rain), Pi'ilani (chief/constructed Maui's roads), maka'āinana (commoner), Kā'uiki (hill above Hāna Bay), āwapuhi ke'oke'o (white ginger), Ka'eokulani (character from local legend), ehu kai (sea spray/scent), Mālualua (North Wind), Hāmoa (beach) mele (song), mālie (calm) Kaihuokala (mountain above Hāna), aokū (rainclouds), Pu'uki'i (island off of Hāna), niu (coconut tree)

GLOSSARY:
HAWAIIAN / ENGLISH

A

ahupua`a - district from mountain to sea
`akepa - upland birds
akua - God/god
alaka`i - leader
aloha kākou - aloha to all including the greeter
`ama`u - all species of fern
`a`ole pilikia - no problem

E

e - used when speaking to someone or giving commands
e hele lālani! - walk in rank!
`ehu - reddish tinge to hair
`eke ho`okalakupua - magic bag
e komo mai - welcome
e kūlia maha! - halt!
e naue i mua! - forward march!

H

hale koa - weedy relative of the mighty koa
hānai - adopted
haole - without breath/white
hāpu`u - large fern tree

hau - upland tree
haupia - coconut dessert
he`e nalu - surf
heiau - temple
hele - go
ho`opau! - stop!
huaka`i pō - night marchers
huhū - anger/trouble
huila - wheel
huna kauā - battle unit

I
`iliahi - general classification of sandalwood trees

K
Kahekili - chief of Maui during reign of Kalaniopu`u and Kamehameha I
Kalaniopu`u - Big Island predecessor of Kamehameha the Great
kahu - priest
kahuna - priest/sorcerer
kalo - taro/poi root
kālua pig - underground baked pork
kanaka - Hawaiian
kapa - Hawaiian cloth
kauā - outcasts
kaukau - food/eat
kēhau - bitter cold

keiki kāne - male child
keiki manu - baby bird
kelekalapa - telegraph
kiawe - hardwood used for charcoal
koa - hardwood upland tree
koa - warrior
koai`e - native koa-like tree used for paddles
koholā - whale
kōlea - migratory shoreline bird/native tree
kōnane - checker/backgammon type game
ko`u kamali`i hulu - my bird children
kukui - candlenut tree/lamp
kūlia - halt
kuleana - responsibillity
kūlolo - coconut sweet

L

lālani - in line, formation
lei pāpale - hat lei
lo`i - kalo patch
lōlō - feeble minded

M

mahi - mahimahi fish
ma kai - toward the sea
mai ka makuakāne a me makuahine - from father and mother

ma`i Pāke - leprosy/Hansen's Disease
maka - eye(s)
makamaka - good friend/highfalutin
makapi`api`a - viscous eye matter
makua - elder
makule - old
māmane - high altitude luguminous tree
mamao iki aku paha - probably farther away
manini - small
ma uka - toward the mountains
mele - song
Mele Kalikimaka - Merry Christmas
Menehune - short people of ancient Hawai`i
mōhailani - heavenly burnt offering to the gods
mo`o - Hawaiian lizard-like monster
mu`umu`u - Mother Hubbard dress

N
no`e no`e - misty rain
**No Ka Loke O Nā Ali`i** - For the Rose of the Chiefs (Hawai`i was the rose)
no ke `ano - for the present

O
`ōhi`a - bottlebrush tree
`ōkole - buttocks (lemu - more polite)
`ōlelo - language

oli - chant
`ono - delicious
`o`opa - lame
`ōpiko - tree/member of the coffee family
`ōpū - stomach

P
Pa`ea - name of Kamehameha the Great
pahu - drum
pakaliona - battalion
paniolo - cowboy
Pāoa - divining rod brought by Pele clan to Hawai`i, also Duke Kahanamoku's name.
papa he`e nalu - surfboard
pāpalei - hat
pau - finished
pauka - squad
pia - beer
**Pi`ilani** - builder of Maui roads in old Hawai`i
pili - grass for building huts
po`i - kalo mash
polū - blue
puka - hole/door
pukaaniani - window
pulu fern - plant with yellow moss at base
pupule - crazy

U
Ua Mau Ke Ea O Ka ʻĀina I Ka Pono - The life of the land is preserved in righteousness.

W
waʻa - canoe
wai - water/drink
waikele - forest
Waiomina - Wyoming
walaʻau - talk story
wēkiu - the top

GLOSSARY:
PIDGIN / ENGLISH

ass - that's
adda - other
bea - beer
eva - ever
da kine - the one, that kind
dat - that
doze - those
dumb do do - idiot
fo - for
gahds - guards

gunfunit - expletive
hea - here
jess - just
kay den - okay then
kinna - kind of
lōlō - crazy
mento - crazy
moa - more
no moa - none left
no try - don't
one - a
only - there are only
peety - pity
pua - poor
slippahs - flip flops
ting - thing
you wen...? - did you?

GLOSSARY: ETHNIC / ENGLISH

Aloha Airlines - former interisland carrier
ampan - Japanese azuki donut
boiled peanuts - Chinese style
bonsai – Japanese sculptured plants
breadfruit - grapefruit size Polynesian staple, baked, broiled, fried, steamed
chicken skin - goose bumps
chow fun - wide noodles prepared in wok
crack seed - Chinese sweetened plum
crown flower - 5 pointed cluster of waxy flowers, white, lavender, East Asia
compadre - friend (Spanish)
David Malo - Hawaiian historian/first graduating class of Lahainaluna
dilly - Dairy Queen ice cream on a stick
50th State Fair - annual Honolulu celebration
flip flops - Japanese slippers
fried soup - fried chow fun
guava jam - spread made from yellow seedy fruit
Helen Parker - famous songwriter *(Akaka Falls)*
jacaranda - tall trees with purple blue corolla, South America
KMVI - first Maui radio station
lychee - oval gelatanous fruit with rough red skin

lū'au plate - kālua pig (substitute laulau), lomi salmon, poi etc.)

manju - Japanese confection made from rice filled with azuki sweet beans

mango - fleshy stone fruit

Matson - interisland/California steamship line

Maui News - daily newspaper

mochie - Japanese rice crackers

mynah birds - medium brown bird with yellow eyes, beak and feet, India

night marchers - zombi-like warriors

Orange Exchange Base - former Hawai'i juice, add 5 cans water, grape too

pandanus - tree with sharp toothed leaves for weaving mats etc.

plumeria - fragrant flower in variety of colors, commonly used for lei

pork in Chinese graveyard - a no no

rosie apple - small Hawaiian variety of apple

saimin - Japanese noodle soup

ti leaf - wide leaf used for cooking and hula skirts

Toscani - Filipino cigar

Trojans - St. Anthony High School nickname

white lady - apparation in 'Īao Valley, statewide

GLOSSARY:
SITES AND LOCATIONS

Sandwich Isles - British name for Hawai`i dedicated to the Earl of Sandwich

MAUI - Island, South Chain

Alexander Sports Complex - former name of Wailuku sports center off Wells Street

Apana's Junkyard - Wailuku business

Banyan Inn - former restaurant across from Banyan Tree, Lahaina

Front Street - main road along ocean, downtown Lahaina

Haleakalā - 10,000 foot Maui volcano

Hamai Appliance - Kahului business

Hāna - East Maui village

Hāna Highway - road from Central Maui to Hāna

Happy Valley - residential area/Wailuku

Ho`okipa - beach, Northeast Maui

`Īao - valley and stream above Wailuku

Ichiki Store - former general merchandise store, Lahaina

Jodo Mission - Buddhist church near Māla Wharf

Kahului - port town, Central Maui

Kahului Fairgrounds - former site of Maui County Fair

Kanahā Pond - swamp area in Kahului

Ka`onohua Gulch - valley near Waikapū, Central Maui

Kaupō - small East Maui village

Kīhei - South Maui village

King Theater - former movie theater, Vineyard St., Wailuku

Kula - upcountry area on lower flank of Haleakalā

Lahaina - old Maui whaling port and former capital of Hawai`i

Lahainaluna - West Maui high school with boarding dept.

Liberty Restaurant - former Front Street eatery, Lahaina

Ma`alae`a - ocean village, Central Maui

Makawao - cattle town, flank of Haleakalā

Māla Wharf - pier in Lahaina

Maui Children's Home - former Maui orphanage, Pā`ia

Maui College - University of Hawai`i, Maui campus

Mill Camp - plantation camp in Wailuku

Olinda Prison - former upcountry minimum security facility

Olowalu - village, a couple of miles south of Lahaina

`Ōma`oma`o Plain - plain between Kahului and Wailuku

Pā`ia - village/bay, East Maui

Pali - steep cliffed shoreline area between Central Maui and Lahaina

Pioneer Mill - sugar mill at Lahaina

Pioneer Inn - hotel/restaurant, Lahaina pier

Pu`umoe Gulch - valley near Waikapū, Central Maui

Pu`unene - mill village in Central Maui

Puamana - beach front before Lahaina

Pū`ūkoli`i - heights above Lahaina

Queen Theater - former movie theater, Front St., Lahaina

Rose Ranch - ʻUlupalakua retreat of monarchy/currently Tedeschi Winery

St. Anthony - school and church, Wailuku

St. Teresa's - Kīhei church

Sprecklesville - village in Northeast Maui

Tasty Crust - Wailuku restaurant

ʻUlupalakua - ranch land, Southeast Maui

Upcountry Maui - usually refers to Haʻikū, Makawao, Kula, and Pukalani

Vineyard Street - street in Wailuku

Wahikuli - heights above Lahaina

Waiheʻe - village, North Maui

Waikapū - village, Central Maui

Wailuku - county seat of Maui

Waineʻe - street in Lahaina

War Memorial Complex - sports center in Wailuku

Wells Park - Wailuku park/first site of Maui County Fair

West Maui Moutains - mountains above Wailuku

OʻAHU - Island, Central Chain

Castle Point - near Diamond Head - named after castle-like house on the bluff

Celestial Bakery - famous store in 1800's downtown Honolulu

Chinatown - downtown Honolulu district

Cunha's - beach area, Waikīkī

Elk's Surf - ocean area off of Elk's Club, Waikīkī

ʻIolani Palace - home of Hawaiian monarchy

Kaimukī - town in South Central Oʻahu

Kalāhuewehe - name for ocean area off Diamond Head

Kāneʻohe - village and asylum, Oʻahu

Kapahulu - village ma uka of Waikīkī

King St. - avenue that runs from downtown south

Koʻolau - montain range above Honolulu

Little Church of Waikīkī - former place of worship/struck by lightning 1876

Makapuʻu - Honolulu surf spot

Mount Lēʻahi/Diamond Head/Diamond Point - extinct crater, South Oʻahu

Public Baths - surf area off of Waikīkī

Queen's - Waikīkī beach area

Royal School - educational institution for monarchy at site of Hawaiʻi State Capitol

St. Louis High School - Catholic school in Kaimukī

University of Hawaiʻi at Manoa - Honolulu campus of UH

Varieties Theater - former venue, downtown Honolulu

Waikīkī - beach and village, South Oʻahu

KAUAʻI - Island, Northern Chain

MOLOKAʻI - Island, Central Chain

Kalaupapa - leper colonly, peninusula, Molokaʻi

Molokaʻi Channel - water crossing between Molokaʻi and Oʻahu

LĀNAʻI - Island, Central Chain

KAHOʻOLAWE - Island, Central Chain

HAWAIʻI - Island, South Chain
Hāwī - Big Island north village
Hāmākua - district, Northeast Hawaiʻi
Hanaipoe - area mauka of Honokaʻa, Hawaiʻi
Honokaʻa - Big Island east village
Hilo - Big Island of Hawaiʻi county seat
Hualālai - large volcano, North Kona
Humuʻula - sheep station, Mauna Kea
ʻIole - Kohala mountain and stream
Kawaihae - village, harbor, Kohala, Hawaiʻi
Kīlauea - active volcano, Southeast Big Island
Kipuʻupuʻu - warrior people and area known for cold rain, Waimea, Hawaiʻi
Kohala - Big Island north district
Kona - Big Island south village
Kukuihaele - village above Waipiʻo Valley, Big Island
Laumaiʻa - 6000 foot land section above Hilo
Mānā - land division on slope of Mauna Kea, Hawaiʻi
Mauna Loa - second highest volcano, Big Island
Mauna Kea - highest volcano, Big Island
Parker Ranch - 185,000 acre ranch, North Hawaiʻi
Pōhakuloa - ranger station on Saddle Road between Mauna Loa and Mauna Kea
Pololū - Big Island north east village and valley
Puna - Big Island southeast village
Puʻuhue - ranch, South Kohala

Pu`uwa`awa`a - land division and peak, Puakō quadrant
UH Hilo - Hilo campus of University of Hawai`i
Waiāpuka - northeast village, Big Island
**Waiki`i** - village, North Central Hawai`i
Waimanu - North Big Island valley
Waipi`o - Big Island east valley

CONTINENTAL U.S.

Cheyenne - Wyoming Capital and site of National Rodeo Championship
Corona Del Mar - near Newport Beach, California
Great Salt Lake - largest salt water lake in West, Utah
Mainland - term used by islanders for continental U.S.
Oakland - East San Francisco Bay city and port
Ogden - Utah city
San Francisco - Northern California city and port
Sierra Nevada - mountains of Northern California

THE HAWAIIAN ISLANDS

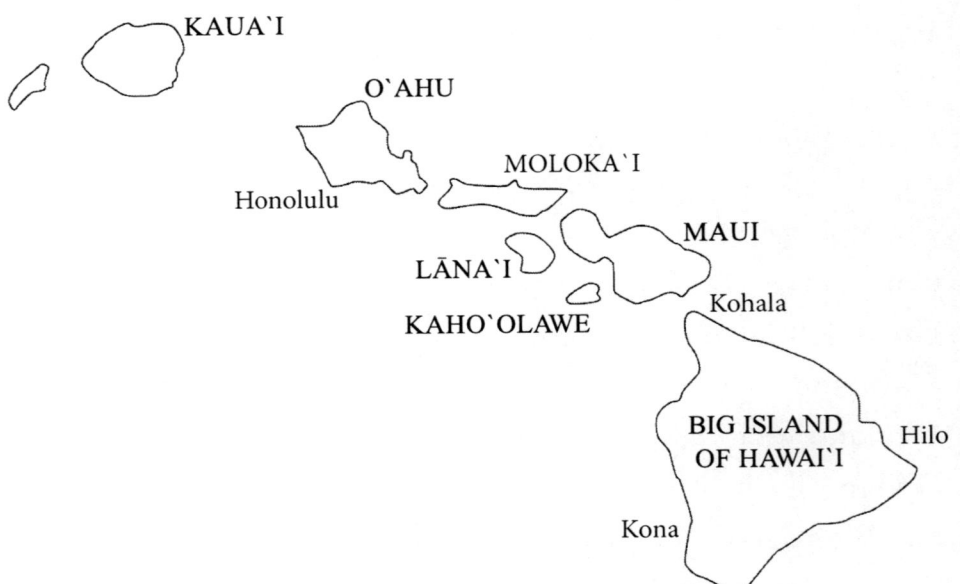

THE ISLAND OF MAUI

THE BIG ISLAND OF HAWAI'I

BY THE SAME AUTHOR

Born and raised on Maui, Wayne Moniz received a B.A. in English and Communications in 1968 from the University of Dayton, Ohio. In 1980, he was awarded an M.A. in Theater Arts - Film from UCLA. In 2005, he received the Cades Award for Literature, Hawaii's most prestigious writing prize. His short story collection of Valley Isle tales won him the Nā Palapala Po`okela 2010 Readers' Choice Book of the Year. Dubbed the "Dean of Maui Playwrights" by The Maui News, Wayne has written works that deal with the people, events, and issues of Hawai`i. They include:

PLAYS

Still Born - Nā Mele o Kaho`olawe
The history and liberation of the island of Kaho`olawe - ©1990. Produced by Maui Community Theater [MCT], 1991. Published by Pūnāwai Press, 2000.

`Ili `Ili
A Hawaiian entertainer and the Spirit of Charles Lindbergh team up to save Hāna from a massive development - ©1994. Produced by MCT, 1991. Published by Pūnāwai Press, 2004.

Children of the Turning Tide
Hawaii's future monarchs as teens at the Royal School - ©1992. Produced by Baldwin Theater Guild [BTG], 1992. Published by Pūnāwai Press, 2000.

Under the Star of Gladness
Three generations of a Portuguese Family and friends in Hawai`i - ©1997. Produced by MCT, 1993. Published by Pūnāwai Press, 2004.

People of the First Year
The first Japanese Christians on Maui - ©1994. Produced by `Īao Congregational Church, 1994.

Steamer Days: The View from Aloha Tower
A romantic romp through a 1938 Honolulu Boat Day with Duke Kahanamoku, Hilo Hattie and Shirley Temple et al - ©1997. Produced by BTG, 1996. Published by Pūnāwai Press, 2007.

Hawaiian Kine Christmas Carol
An 1889 Sprecklesville Mill kine version of the Dickens' classic - ©1997. Produced by MCT, 1997.

Kamapua`a - The Exploits of the Pig god
©1997, Produced by Hawaii Leadership Conference for Nā Kumu `Ōlelo Hawai`i, Maui Community College, 1997.

Pele and Hi`iaka: Sisters of Fire
The odyssey of the Pele Family and Hi`iaka's journey to escort Lohi`au from Kaua`i to Halema`uma`u - ©1997.

Tandy!
The libretto of an opera based on the rise and fall of Hāna born opera singer, Tandy MacKenzie - ©1997. Published by Pūnāwai Press, 2007.

Hibiscus Pomade
`60s musical when Hawaiian music met rock `n roll with Lucky, Aku and the KPOI Boys—©2002. Produced by BTG, 2004. Published by Pūnāwai Press, 2007.

Only the Morning Star Knows: In Search of Kamehameha
The search for the bones of Kamehameha leads King Kalākaua into the mind of Hawaii's greatest monarch - ©2003.

`Īao: Where We Walk Through Rainbows
The stories of the sacred valley from prehistory to modern times - ©2004.

SHORT STORIES

Under Maui Skies and Other Stories
©2010. Koa Books.

Kepaniwai
©1969. Published in <u>University of Dayton Literary Journal</u>, 1969. On display at the Hilo Tsunami Museum.

Aloha ʻOe, E Kuʻuipo.
©2006. Published in <u>Maui Community College Literary Magazine</u>, 2006.

Under Maui Skies.
©2007. Published in <u>Hawaii Weavers of Tales</u>. National Writers Association—Honolulu Chapter, 2008.

POEMS, MUSIC AND LYRICS

Wailuku, 1957
(Poem) ©2006. Published in <u>Literary Breeze from Hawaiʻi</u>. National Writers Association—Honolulu Chapter, 2006.

Maui Moon Blues
(Music and Lyrics) ©1990. From his drama, *Still Born: Nā Mele o Kahoʻolawe.*

Hibiscus Pomade
(Music and Lyrics) ©2002. From his musical comedy, *Hibiscus Pomade.*

The Makawao Fourth of July Parade
(Music and Lyrics) ©2003.

Ke One o Ka Puʻu Hale Nani
(Lyrics) Music by Pekelo Cosma ©2008.

FILMS

The Chair Resistance
(Producer). West Valley Productions, ©1980.

Laugh Trax
Producer. (Segment Director). West Valley Productions, ©1981.

Standing in the Shadows
(Producer). West Valley Productions, ©1982.

Aloha `Oe, E Ku`uipo
(Screenplay), ©2008.

ABOUT THE ARTIST

Joseph Aspell is an artist who lives in San Francisco. He has a BA in Literature, an MA in Art History, and an MA in Painting. His sculptures have been commissioned for churches and universities across the U.S.

See his amazing work at: josephaspellstudio.com

PŪNĀWAI PRESS
-e pua`i wale mai ana-

Pūnāwai Press publishes dramas, screenplays, short stories, novels,
poetry, non fiction and song lyrics
about the people, events, and issues of Hawai`i.

To get more information,
or obtain an AUDIO BOOK, write to:

Pūnāwai Press
1812 Nani St.
Wailuku, Maui
Hawai`i 96793

To purchase more copies of BEYOND THE REEF,
go online to Amazon.com
For more about the book and author, Google:
Beyond the Reef: Stories of Maui in the World/Wayne Moniz
To purchase copies of Wayne's previous book,
UNDER MAUI SKIES AND OTHER STORIES
Go to: KoaBooks.com
UnderMauiSkies.com
Amazon.com

CPSIA information can be obtained at www.ICGtesting.com
Printed in the USA
LVOW081727100512

281226LV00005B/14/P